*The Baby Makers*
# The Emu Club

*Table of Contents*

# Acknowledgement

*In writing this novel, I could not have done so without the computer technical support and cover design by my sister Melody Moss.*

*With the editing of the book, I must give a big thanks to Sally Montgomery for correcting my poor spelling.*

*My biggest heartfelt thanks go to my wife Stephanie. Without your permission and understanding, I would never have been able to write this book.*

*A lifetime of thanks.*

*To you the reader I thank you for investing this book.*

James Taylor March 2016.

*theemuclub@gmail.com*

*Preface*

In this book you will follow a eight year journey of Michael and Connie Reid.  Their quest for a baby begins in love with a bright future together.  Going by the tests and medical evidence IVF is the only choice, or is it?

In reading this confronting book, you too may discover that sometimes you need to, "Be careful of what you wish and pray for."

During the year 2011 in Australia and New Zealand their was 40,696 cycles of IVF. Of live births achieved that year the rate was 17% per cycle.
This is the harsh reality of IVF.

In Australia the out of pocket expenses for a ICSI cycle can be as high as $3,820.00  This can be a high cost, with other specialist and testing fees as well.

This can place a burden of pressure and stress, on those involved to "Achieve a little miracle."

This is only one of the many IVF stories untold.

"Hearing a hundred times is not as good as seeing one."
Traditional Chinese saying.

## Chapter 1

*THE EMU CLUB*

It is the middle of the morning in the main bedroom, of the Reids' rented home. Standing next to the bed, Michael ponders what he has to do next. Connie sticks her head through the bedroom doorway, looks at her husband.
"I will wait for you in the car, dear."

Upon hearing the back door close, he opens his eyes. Without hesitation, he opens the top drawer of his bed side table and finds the two items he needs. Unscrewing the jar lid, he carefully places it on the side table within easy reach.

Picking up the magazine Connie brought for him, he flicks through the pages until he sees the image, he needs. Slowly at first he feels his penis harden until he knows that he is ready to stroke it. The image of two ladies spread out before him, helps as he unzips his pants, lowers his underwear and starts to masturbate.

The pleasure of knowing that after 5 days, relief is close by. Fighting the feeling to ejaculate, Michael resists and picking up the magazine with one hand. Masturbates harder while flicking through the magazine until images of woman having sex, makes him loose focus.
He realizes he's about to ejaculate, before he can grab the open jar. The first stream of semen explodes out and does an arch and lands on Connie's pillows. Quickly grabbing the jar he forces his erect penis into the jar for the remainder of his ejaculation.

After looking at the semen in the jar he carefully screws the lid on tight. Then he pulls up his underwear, zips his pants up and puts the jar in his jacket pocket.

Walking to the other side of the bed, seeing the semen and turns Connie's pillow over. Then checking himself in the bedroom mirror he heads out towards the back door.

He remembers to slip the magazine under his own pillows. This, IVF couple have no idea how costly that first missed stream of semen would turn out to be.

Not speaking, while Inside Nissan Bluebird station wagon until on Punt Road Richmond, 70 minutes later in the morning.  It is in the early March and autumn is now underway.

Connie is driving along Punt Road in Richmond, looking at the time on the dashboard Michael speaks tensely with a slight panic in the tone of his voice.

"How much further to the clinic"?

"Your doctor said we have an hour before bloody quality is affected."

Connie gives Michael an annoyed sideways glance and replies, "Less than a couple of streets away.  Relax I know what I am doing."

Michael answers with,

"What's that mean?"

Without answering the question Connie announces as she indicates.

There's the clinic ahead, I've learnt I can park in the next lane way behind the bookshop, free for two hours."

Without listening Michael looks at the huge nearby construction site, with its cranes in amazement and asks Connie.

"What's going on there?"

Connie informs a puzzled Michael,

"Shop's and apartments, dear."

Level 3, is a busy place with the andrology department with its big reception desk. It is filled with men and woman, waiting patiently. It is the attractive assistant whom Michael first approaches asking where and how to hand over his jar for testing.

Directing him to a man at another counter, he sighs reluctantly walking towards the line to do the handover. Ever so efficiently without looking up he checks the details on the jar paperwork before saying;
"That will be fine."

Michael was a lot quicker walking away from the andrology clinic to where Connie was waiting. With a slight laugh Connie says,
"You are not the only bloke to wank into a jar today." To which Michael responds, "At least I'm still being paid for it. What floor is this specialist on?"
"Six dear."
The quality of the fixtures and fittings always surprises all new patients. A life-size copy of Vincent Van Goughs "Flowers" is the main standout painting in the waiting room. Two other couples are also waiting to see Dr Sloob. Michael sits down in the leather lounge chair closest to the magazine rack, which, to his disappointment, looks filled with pregnancy and parental magazines. Hunting through, he settles on a beach wear magazine. Looking up and seeing Connie at the front desk going through and chatting happily with the receptionist regarding the paperwork. They smile at each other as he wonders how he could make up his morning appointments without Brian his newspaper sales manager finding out. Connie returns to sit next to Michael to go through the paperwork given by the receptionist staff.
"The test this and his consultation today are bulked billed, each consultation from now on is pay as you go."

Michael looks up from the bikini models and replies,
"Is that all?"
Fearing what was to come next.
"They freeze each semen sample, storage costs are four hundred dollars, every six months!"
Putting her hand to her chest Connie looks at her husband.
"Each cycle costs between $660 to $1450, depending or not, if you go ISCI."

Outside in the corridor of Dr Ivan Sloob, both Michael and Connie are walking towards his rooms. They automatically stop when they see the photographs of babies and personal letters of thanks to Dr Sloob. Halting and temporarily overcome by the framed photos, cards and letters from couples who had IVF success with Dr Ivan as their specialist. The receptionist stops by the door and knowingly waits as another couple, admire other couples holding their new born babies.
After knocking on Dr Sloob's door she smiles and tells them.
"You can go in now, he is ready for you both." Connie said as tears start to swell in her eyes,
"There must be over 50 cards, photos and letters."
To which the receptionist smiles and says,
"Hopefully soon you too will send us some baby's photos."

Dr Ivan Sloob's medical rooms are large but very practical.  Behind his desk on the wall are all his medical certificates and his London medical degree.  The solid wooden desk is sparse except for a computer, a writing pad and a photo of his wife holding their grandson. When they are shown into Dr Sloob's rooms both are surprised by just how plain looking Dr Sloob looked and dressed.

Now, Mr & Mrs Reid are quietly seated facing Dr Sloob. Like their children's school principal Dr Sloob did not speak for over a minute. He carefully reads through Connie's medical file and the couple's family histories. His first question catches both off guard.

"Why do you want to have a baby together? I can see that both of you have had children from your previous marriages?"

It was Michael who responded first.

"Yes we do have children from our first spouses, I two girls and Connie two boys and a girl. We are called the Brady Bunch but we both desire to complete our blended bunch, with our own baby together.

Looking up from the notes Dr Sloob continues his questioning.

"I see you have only been married less than a year."

Connie who has bit her tongue, until now has joined the conversation.

"That is true but we have been together over three years."

Dr Sloob, comments looking up from the medical files.

"I see that both of you have had medical procedures, you Michael a vasectomy then a reversal?"

The focus from Dr Sloob's gaze is now directly on the couple in front of him and how they answer. Michael corrects Dr Sloob.

"That's true but the surgeon was unable to rejoin the left testicle."

Anticipating the next question;

"The vasectomy was seven years ago, the reversal January last year."

Dr Sloob now relaxes back into his chair, nods and says, "I see."

Then adding his own unexpected warning to the couple.

"Even though this is 1995 and medical IVF science has improved immensely. Alpha/Stork IVF cannot give you a 100% guarantee of having a baby.

If our SMET test confirms what I believe that if you choose IVF, ISCI is one of the options I do recommend. You could keep trying naturally but, your time options are then limited."

Lowering her gaze Connie answers with determination.

"We know, and are prepared to try and follow it through."

Satisfied, Dr Sloob finishes with speaking with them as a couple.

"Good now Connie, my medical staff will ring you later in the week to confirm your menstrual cycle dates and inform you of the andrology results for Michael."

Dr Ivan Sloob then indicates today's meeting was now over. Both look at each other and both are too shocked to speak to each other until they reached their car.

## Chapter 2

Noticing the quiet home as he walks into the kitchen, all the children are home quietly seated while Connie starts dinner. Even Amber the cat is inside quietly watching everyone.  It is third day after their IVF visit. It is approaching six o'clock as Michael first notices the cold stares from his daughters. Thinking quickly, he deems it best to give a hello kiss to Connie first.  From the way she turns her head all he could say was, "What's wrong?"

"I received a phone call today from Dr Sloob's rooms.  They say they want you to do another, you know test as the first one was very poor."

All Michael can say is "Oh, I see."

Connie snaps back. "No you don't see that Julie and Jason both have school camps that need to be paid for."

"And?" Fearing again what would be said next. Connie puts down the wooden spoon she is holding and looks at Michael with tears in her eyes.

"I got my period today."

It is a very quiet family dinner.

It is the middle of the following week and Michael is again in the main bedroom alone.  Now this time Michael has not ejaculated as required.  He is determined and says to himself, "Do it correctly this time."
Quietly he manages to get all his seamen into the jar. The other hassle's he is now facing is the morning's peak traffic ahead. With his own car in for a major service, he has to take Connie's Bluebird wagon then drop the kids at school and Connie off to work.  He hears Connie's hair dryer stop, so Michael opens the door and sticks his head into the two way bathroom, informing Connie.

"We have to go."

Calling out to the kids to hurry up to go to school, does not improve his anxiety or nervous fear of another bad test result.  The future cost and intrusive nature of the IVF tests is causing stress on Connie too.

Deep inside he always regretted having the vasectomy demanded by his first wife.  What made him heartbroken was that she fell pregnant to another man six months after she walked out on their marriage.  It was Michaels plan to go see the urologist about having a reversal done.  He realized that every time he saw a baby boy part of him felt lacking.  Connie wanted to raise a baby with a man she could trust and knew would not leave her.  It is Anna, Michael's youngest daughter who hops into the station wagon first, with a frown on her face.

"What's the matter Princess?"

Ann's sudden outburst surprise's her father by its depth of feeling.

"It's Connie, dad. She snaps at us kids all the time. Sometimes I can't stand it and wish I was living with mum.  Sandra and I hate her mood swings."

Before Michael can respond the rest of the family came and hoped into the car. Connie sitting next to him with the four kids squished into the rear seat; all grateful it was only a short trip to school. Hopefully today's test results would lift Connie's mood. So Michael thinks as he starts the car.

Driving the Bluebird wagon in heavy traffic on Punt Road Richmond, the traffic is heavy and already it is 9.40 in the morning. Michael realizes that it needs a service and the handbrake does not work at all. To make matters worse he is crawling along Punt Road and his sperm is over one hour old. For reasons Michael could not explain, he takes the jar out of his pocket and examines it while driving. Caught unawares the car in front stops suddenly, which he sees just in time.

The sudden jamming on the brakes causes him to drop the jar. This rolls on to the floor and somehow manages to jam itself, under the brake pedal. Out of a sudden real fear of Connie and abstinence again, he frantically searches with one hand to remove the stuck jar. Quickly total panic kicks in as he sees ahead the traffic stop for the lights at the Punt Road oval intersection. Applying the handbrake is useless, so he overtakes all the cars on the inside bicycle lane, avoiding using the brakes at all. He literally closes his eyes as he drives past some cyclists then through the red lights at the intersection. Somehow the other drivers avoid hitting him, through a major traffic intersection, against the red lights. With his mouth wide open now a vacant parking spot somehow appears near Alpha/Stork IVF. Placing the automatic into neutral, he steers the car as it gently rolls into the spot.  It takes Michael a good two minutes to stop feeling sick, before he can remove the jar.

His sample is 100 minutes old before it is handed over for testing.

*Chapter 3*

Connie & Michael are sitting down together alone, outside in the courtyard.  Connie holding the letter rereads it again.

"It says that due to the high abnormal forms percentage, 89% and the low motility count." Taking a sip of her wine she continues reading unsure if she wants too.

"This test will also be conducted using donor mucus to examine the motility percentage of the sperm. The letter also says that the samples tested so far showed high IgG sperm anti-bodies."

Connie asks Michael, "What are sperm anti-bodies?"

Taking another sip of her wine, as she continues to read the letter.

"The sperm motility enhancement test will be the evidence on which Alpha/Stork IVF will commence any future, IVF treatment once the tests have been completed."

With a concerned look on her face she continues to read.

"That any commencement of IVF is subject to written permission by Mr & Mrs Reid with Alpha/Stork IVF Pty Ltd. Enclosed are authority payment forms. Please read, sign and return to our office. Attached is a semen analysis form for the Alpha/Stork andrology laboratory."

Michael finishes his cup of tea nods, kisses Connie on her head and goes inside to wash the dishes.  That night Connie drinks her wine outside by herself holding onto the letter.  Later on, Michael sees her come into the home heading straight to the bedroom wiping her eyes.

It is the following week with both Connie & Michael waiting together at the andrology laboratory with Michael wanting to speak to the assistant behind the counter regarding how and where he is to do the sperm motility enhancement test. The andrology assistant again takes the form, but this time comes back and gives him two jars.

Michael is quick to ask,
"Why two jars?"
The assistant replies,
"That is because this sperm motility enhancement test, requires a split load."
With fear showing in his voice,
"What is a split load?"

Now the assistant, enjoying himself, leans on the counter and informs Michael and Connie quietly that.
"It's the first stream of your ejaculation which is to go into the first jar.  Any other streams of ejaculated semen are to go into the second jar."
Michael now shocked bursts out with his voice raised,
"How am I to manage that?"
The assistant now winks at Connie and says,
"I am sure you'll work it out. Others do."
Now he is grinning. Connie is quick to inform her husband that, "You are on your own in there dear."
Then she turns away and quickly grabs a woman's magazine before sitting down.  Michael feels uncomfortable thinking that people are watching as he goes into the men's private room.
In the small room the only furnishings are a leather armchair, side table with a television.  With a VCR recorder on top which looks damaged. The girlie magazines look used like the television.
Taking the two jars out of his jacket pockets, Michael looks at them as he unscrews the lids and places them on top of the VCR recorder.  Having never masturbated sitting down, he can only wonder as to how any man could wank himself, in that leather armchair.  Deciding to continue to stand up, Michael picks up the magazines and starts to look at them.
Browsing through the magazines the Playboy and soft core issues did nothing to improve his mood and the

non responsive penis.  After a couple more minutes of no action, he looks at the other magazines.

The one which catches his eye is a German issue which at least shows explicit nude women.  Now he feels a stir from his groin area, undoing his belt and fly zip. He then lowers his underpants taking his semi-soft penis and starts to stroke it. Again this time a photo of a woman having sex brings Michael to his ejaculation. With a controlled determination he ejaculates the first stream into the first jar.  Holding both jars, Michael just puts his penis into the second jar as a female voice calls out someone's name loudly, knocking on the door. Completely startled, he drops both jars.

Twenty minutes later while on Punt Road Richmond, Connie is driving as Michael has refused.  Connie this time is trying to lift the mood of her husband.  Who quietly observes to himself the now built floors of the shop & apartment complex are up to six.

"Look, I spoke to the assistant at the counter and explained what happened today and they were very understanding."

Michael is unresponsive and looks out the window.

"They apologized and said that it should not have happened. There was not enough for the test which they will freeze anyway, so they gave me another form."

"Which means that I have to take time off work to do the bloody test again?"

This time Connie responds by informing Michael.

"Really? If you didn't have balls of straw we would not have to do bloody IVF"

Soon realizing what she said Connie adds,

"I am sorry."

All Michael can say is, "Me too."

But he is not sorry about the test; it is something else bothering him.  It is then Michael thinks that this IVF is beginning to change Connie and himself.

How lately he started wondering about the true price of having a baby by IVF.

### Chapter 4

It is seven days later and again in the andrology laboratory waiting room.  This time the attractive female assistant is at the counter to take the form and give Michael the two jars.  Visually checking the waiting room before going to the men's collection room, Michael enters, this time prepared.  Ignoring the clinics supply of magazines, he takes out his own two new magazines which he purchased from an adult bookstore that morning.  With a new found sense of self justification Michael, starts to easily masturbate and enjoy it.  These magazines are more explicit in material than anything, he had seen before.  He enjoys looking at women having sex with many partners and not hiding their enjoyment.  Seeing the photo's helps bring him to the point of his secret satisfaction.  Michael is now satisfied and looking forward to the next time.

He is becoming very dissatisfied with Connie's no  to anything, that would not result in a possible pregnancy.  All he wanted was easy sex with his wife without the complications and temperature charts. The correct times and days were so important now, so unlike before they started trying to have a baby by IVF.

It is now the end of April and the extended families are together at the courtyard area outside to gather for Sandra's 12$^{th}$ birthday.

It is Michael's father, Bob who approaches and asks Anna how things are going.  After briefly speaking with Anna, he approaches Michael.

"What is this IVF doctor's treatment that I hear your doing?"

Michael responds after thinking carefully.

"Yes Connie and I start it next month, with Alpha/Stork IVF."

Looking directly at him, his father asks,
"Can you afford it and do you really need to do it? You already have your hands full with five kids."
By this time Connie has somehow managed to stand next to Michael without him being aware.
"Yes we can, were going ahead with it."
Connie gives Michael a look then shifts her focus to Anna who becomes visibly upset and goes inside.

Bob asks,
"Will you still be able to buy a home this year?"
Michael responds to Connie's prompting by answering,
"Look dad, our landlord is OK if we stay on for another 12 months.
"And that's fine by us; we have it under control,"
Connie stated.
"We know what we are doing, even if others don't."
Humbled by the onslaught of emotional determination of words from Connie, Bob looks for Anna but changes the subject to football and their beloved Carlton football club.
"Are you planning on going to see some Carlton games this year?"
With this conversation underway Connie leaves and goes inside to speak to Anna.

### Chapter 5

It is now the middle of May.  Now they are going ahead with IVF.  Today is day 10 of Connie's menstrual cycle.  This is the third time Michael has come to Punt Road in Richmond this month.  One couple's counseling session with the clinic and the other one was yesterday for a seminal analysis. They are taking turns in driving; Michael now notices the slab being poured for the 10$^{th}$ floor of the unit construction site. You can tell that winter is well underway. They go to the 4$^{th}$ floor as directed.

Now it is time for Connie to be nervous. As previously advised Connie has been only taking the tablet Clomit. When they have finished the information session.

The tests and scans they were told would,
"Take a little while."

Connie follows the nurse into a treatment room to get changed. Not being one to sit around easily Michael decides to head out and go for a walk. Braving the chilly weather in his suit, he takes off to find a coffee shop away from the clinics. Michael is definitely unsure of his feelings about the procedures that Connie has had to put her body through to do IVF. Their daily talk and bedroom talk was mostly about what they had to do next.  He felt guilty and remorseful that Connie had to do the "Hard part."

Seeking a coffee/cake shop Michael stumbles into a small but warm coffee shop called "Heathers" on Bridge Road. Quickly realizing it is run by a woman who, from the newspapers and magazines articles cut out and rainbows on the walls is opinionated and willing to share it.

After ordering his coffee, Michael is prepared to settle in and quietly read the mornings newspapers and screen any work calls.

It isn't too long before Heather starts to make small conversation as she forms an opinion of her new customer.

"You look worried dear," she says looking directly at Michael. Surprised, Michael starts to say something but Heather holds up her right hand.

"It is OK, dear. Tell me when you are ready."

Michael is going to tell this lady to "Buzz Off," but a thought strikes him. No, this lady whom Michael does not know is going to get the truth.

Even if it hurts to admit the truth,

"My wife is having an IVF test at the Alpha/Stork clinic. I am not 100% sure she should."

"I knew it, I knew it."

Giving him a biscuit, Heather adds.

"You have walked in the right door, call it cosmic but sit there and listen to what I know and believe."

Only the mobile phone call from Connie telling him that she is ready takes him away from what he is being told. If he had any doubts before now, he hopes to share them with Connie. Michael finishes his second coffee says his goodbye and hurries to walk back to the clinic. Connie is waiting by the entrance of the building to shield herself from the May weather.

Michael asks,

"How did it all go?"

"I couldn't believe it. Here I am laying flat on my back with my legs in the air, Susan and Brook the nurses were lovely but the doctor just mumbles his instructions!"

Michael decides not to say anything to Connie at this time. Placing his arm around his wife, he can see the stress of the procedures in her face. "I see," was all he can think of to say. Now he is too afraid to speak to Connie about her mental health and behavior towards the children.

Was Heather correct?

*Chapter 6*

It is a Sunday night but it is a cold but clear early June night.  Michael is driving his car and has gone to some shopping and hire a couple of VHS movies for the kids. He notices a gathering of cars at a primary school as they drive past and wonders what's going on. He has his two daughters in the car with him.

"Dad, that's where my teacher goes to Church, Ms Casey told me she has been going there for a couple of months."

Then with an annoyed tone, Anna informs her dad.

"She said she spoke to Connie and would pray for you both in your having a baby. Connie and some other mums hold these secret talks and I keep getting foul looks from Mrs Parker. I wish she would pray for Connie to stop being grumpy."

Both girls nodding together in unison.

"Girls it's not as bad as it seems. Once we get through these doctors visits it will get better, I promise."
Michael is not sure if he told a lie to the girls and himself as well.

Michael and both girls arrived home, coming in the back door with a bag full of VHS movies to watch during the week. There is minimal lighting in the house and Michael wonders why.  While turning some lights on he finds Connie sitting alone in the darkened lounge room drinking. As Connie's children were not due back until the morning from an access visit with their father. Michael tells the girls, "Go to your room," having decided to tackle Connie on her grumpiness and drinking.

"Why do you have the house in darkness and why are you drinking before dinner?"

"Why this and why that.  Why don't you grow some balls Mr Straw man? Cook your own fucking dinner."

Angry now, Michael loses some physical self control as he closes the curtains and turns on the lamp.

"I don't understand why you are acting this way.
 What is wrong Connie?"
"I will tell you what's wrong, that I have to have scans, tablets and those fucking needles."
Holding on to her wine glass, she adds looking directly at him.
"When it's your problem; not mine."
"Now hang on a minute here, I told you about my vasectomy when I met you and what the doctors said about any more possible children."
"All I know is that I was fine before."
Now seeing the tears in her eyes as she looks down to the floor.
"I got my period today I did not even reach 25 days in my own cycle, thanks to these needles and procedures."
Now Michael understands and says no more. Without speaking he comes to his wife and holds her. Connie starts sobbing and Michael gently sits her down again on the couch.  Without saying anything he leaves the lounge room and starts to prepare dinner.  It is all he could think of doing.
By the time dinner is ready, Connie was lying on the couch quietly sleeping.  She is clearly not well and never touched her dinner.

*Chapter 7*

By now it is late November 1995, with Connie and Michael failing to fall pregnant by IVF procedures within Connie's natural menstrual cycle. The andrology tests still indicate high IgG sperm anti-bodies with abnormal counts exceeding 75% every test. Alpha/Stork IVF gave their assessment and medical notes to Princess Margret's Reproductive Biology Clinic. They were released from Alpha/Stork because of the couple's inability to keep up the payments for treatment with the clinic. They are seated in a U shape arrangement with Dr Heath together. Dr Heath is again reading the couple's medical file which was shared by Alpha/Stork.

Connie has admitted to Dr Heath over the telephone, that they had missed holidays and social outings by saving the money for the tests, scans and medications. They are upset knowing they just could not afford to try ISCI with Alpha/Stork IVF, with nothing to show for all the alternatives. Connie is becoming bitter as she felt it impacted on her menstrual cycles. They both are anxious that it was public hospital which put them on a long waiting list. Dr Heath is the senior registrar of the Reproductive Biology Unit, very quickly Connie, felt at ease with this doctor.

Michael could see some cards, photo's and thank you notes but it was obvious that they were personal and not for public display. The waiting room had a very different smell with no flowers, scent sticks and the reading magazines were all about Princess Diana.

"Michael, I can see from the Alpha/Stork andrology laboratory that your abnormal forms were between 79 to 89%."

Pausing to think how to say it and looking directly at them both.

"Also on your percentage not once did any test get to 75% motility.  Do you understand what this means with your semen tests?"

No one speaks as Connie stares out the window before looking back at Dr Heath.

Now Dr Heath turns her attention to Connie.
"Connie with the changes to your menstrual cycle as you describe, I think we will book you in for a possible endometrial biopsy and have a look at your tubes, so to speak. If you don't fall pregnant this year. Your youngest daughter was born in 1987. Is that correct?"
Connie answered with a "Yes" unsure of where this conversation was going.
"Your own family doctor has written that he twice consulted with you for possible endometriosis but no treatment was ever taken.  No other pregnancies since then?"
"I did not have sex with a man for over 4 years, after her birth, how could I?"
Rolling her eyes and crossing her arms looking away while seated.
Now it is Michael who asks,
"Excuse me but getting back to my sperm tests.  I was on medication for chronic tonsillitis during, I think all the tests. Also could the antibiotics affect the sperm count or quality?"
With a certain medical confidence Dr Heath answers.
"I am going to order a sperm motility enhancement test for you Michael closely looking at the penetration in a cervical mucus test. Any chance of medication affecting the results is very doubtful,"
Speaking softly, as she ends the consultation.

"You both have some thinking to do as I think as a couple you are suitable for ISCI, or direct injection using donor sperm.  Michael, if you have not ejaculated for 3 days minimum you can do the test here today, so I can get things underway for you both."

Michael reluctantly takes the form, knowing that it was true.  He does not have his magazines with him.

"It is lovely to meet you both and I will write to you as soon as the test results come back from the andrology lab."

Connie, afraid asks one final question while looking at Michael.

"How long is the waiting list to go on the program?"

Dr Heath answers by touching Connie's hand.

"Six to nine months is the average but over the Christmas break, we have gaps that become available." Looking directly at Connie who has closed her eyes as Dr Heath finishes with,

"I'll see what I can do."

They both say "Thank You" as they leave the room.

They have to get the lift down to the basement level to get to the andrology laboratory at Princess Margret's hospital. Upon presenting the test form Michael is given two jars and a sealed bag to put them in. He is again directed to the private room to do the semen test.  This time Connie does not wait. She leaves Michael and goes straight to her car to wait for him. Alone in the room with its bright lights being the only modern alteration to what Michael believes was a former storage/cleaners room. Again he wonders who furnished the room with a clearly old chair, table and a television.

With a VHS recorder that was older and more broken looking than his previous testing room.  Flicking through the men's magazines does little to get him started.

Then, noticing some of the magazines were as good as he had at home, these helped him start to masturbate. From looking at the Crazy Country Chicks magazine and the explicit photos he is ready to ejaculate. Until he notices the middle pages of the magazine are stuck together. Feeling suddenly sick he drops the magazine. It takes another two minutes before he was ready to start again.  After Michael knows that unless he has a baby, he would keep these incidents to himself.  Grateful at least, that there is no one at the collection counter when he drops the sealed bag off. Michael goes to the car, hoping never to wank in one of those test rooms again.  Now he feels very angry and dirty with a growing disgust within that he cannot explain, even to himself.

Connie is driving the Bluebird station wagon and has driven across Melbourne and turned right on to Punt Road.  Two things they both notice is the new Alpha/Stork sign billboard sign with a new born baby on it urging unsuccessful  couples to try IVF. The second and slightly more unsettling sight is that the shops/apartment complex is at about the 19th floor with glass windows and internal fitting out clearly underway. Connie has been playing a song by "Heart."

Michael wondered if Connie knew as they drove past the construction site. A sign of her frustration perhaps, his answers come quickly.


"If today's test results are terrible, I would like to try donor semen as they do an injection when the ovulation cycle is right."

Giving Michael a quick glance, Connie says.

"I would not have to have any injections or ISCI type of procedures; you don't have to do anything."

Michael is unhappy about that and, looking directly at Connie, lets fly with sudden inner anger.

"I thought that WE were trying for a baby. Any kid would not even look like me, what if it's a black or brown kid, or ugly.  I believe we should continue with the IVF".

Knowing he now hated semen tests and how quickly IVF was controlling their lives.

"Now you're being an arsehole. They match the donor father in looks and height. At least the sperm donor will have balls that work straw man."

Michael suddenly lets fly with his right hand and hits Connie hard on the arm while she is driving. It is the first time he has hit Connie.
They continue the drive home in silence. Connie is to upset to speak with the radio turned off.

### Chapter 8

The follow up semen analysis test shows abnormal morphology to be 81% with borderline motility of 38%. The devastation and the realization for Michael that the test showed 100% IgG sperm antibodies to be 100% on the head and tail. The results in the letter from Dr Heath were getting worse for Michael and placing more pressure with Connie. The letter also confirmed that for a donor injection option was available in late January 1996, with a donor match. They are seated again with Dr Heath on a hot late January day in her office.

"You both are well aware that with all the numerous semen analysis tests done by both us and Alpha/Stork IVF, is that you, Michael, are a medically infertile male."

Michael can only stare at the floor.

"As Connie is in her late 30's should emphasize the point that if you want to conceive as a couple then donor sperm or ISCI are your best chances."

Looking at Connie, Dr Heath continues with conviction.

"If you do, say, two donor sperm cycles and do not conceive. Connie, we will do a procedure on you to make sure everything is patent and clear. Before I, or Princess Margret's Reproductive Unit would consider ISCI."

Dr Heath opens a file and, reading from it, informs them both "I have checked the donor files and I can see a possible suitable match from a donor who has similar height, skin complexion and hair to Michael."

Sitting in the U shape arrangement, this time Dr Heath is leaning closer to Michael, who is visibly uncomfortable with the conversation.

"Michael I can see that you are uncomfortable with donor sperm but close to 20% or more of couples are using donor sperm or donor eggs. It is true that we have a shortage of male donors but, in your case, I believe we have a suitable match. So if you are in agreement, Connie I will give you the cycle dates charts for you to record the first day of your menstrual cycle to begin with."

Looking at Michael and Connie before adding, not seeing that the body language of the couple said otherwise.

"Are we in agreement to do donor sperm injection then?"

Connie says firmly while looking at her husband,

"Yes we are.  As Michael looks away all he could do is nod a yes.

"Great. Then all you have to do is read the confidentiality clauses, sign some paperwork and your under way."

Only Connie is happy that day, Michael decides to ask for unplanned sex that night. Since he is being forced to do donor sperm he might as well please himself, when he felt like it.

*Chapter 9*

Having arranged with Connie to pick up the three youngest children from Our St Mark's primary school, Michael is casually chatting to one of the fathers, when he is approached by Ms Casey, Anna's grade 4 teacher from the previous year.

"Hello, Michael.  How are you?  I hope you and Connie were able to have a nice Christmas break with the children."

"Well yes and no.  We did not go to Lorne camping as planned as we had to do other stuff," Michael admits.

"Yes I spoke to Anna while on yard duty; she told me that Connie is again doing IVF today, about which she is not happy."

Well yes, Connie is now on her way home from Princess Margret's IVF Reproductive Unit as we speak."

"It must be a real struggle to manage doing that with five children."

"It will be a lot easier, having switched from the private clinics.  The fees for any cycles were too much; we just could not afford it."

"I will pray for you both to achieve your hearts and families desire."

"Thank you."

What Ms Casey said troubles him, as Anna slowly approaches her father after leaving the classroom. Michael turns back to Ms Casey and asks his own question.

"Anna tells me that you go to a church at the state primary school on the highway, on a Sunday night?"

"Yes that is correct Michael. You are more than welcome to join us and the service starts at 6 pm.  Bring the girls also."

"I might just do that."

Michael says, now wondering as he walks away with Anna what on earth prompted him to agree to that.

It is the Sunday evening and Michael has taken Sandra & Anna with him out to the local state primary school.  Connie is dozing on the couch again as her three children are away on access until the following morning. The girls are eating the last slices of the take away pizza for dinner, as they arrive.  Michael parks out front of the school and follows other arrivals to what appears to be the meeting room.  It is a warm summer night and most attendees are casually dressed.  At the door, ready to greet them, is Ms Casey.

"Welcome and you are all very lucky tonight as we have a very special guest speaker, who we are blessed to have visit us."

Seeing the hesitation in Michael and the girls' faces, Ms Casey was quick to put them at ease.

"Please in here; call me Louise and may I introduce my fiancé Robert Preston."

Anna gives her father a surprised look which would not be, the only one for the night.  The girls obviously had no idea about her fiancé. They warmly shakes hands, make some small talk as the small three piece band starts to play a church song that is unknown to them.  Quickly directed to take a seat, suddenly Michael feels very uncertain as to what he got them into for the night.

The first fifteen or so minutes are completely strange to Michael yet it does not frighten him.  It is very different from any Catholic service he attended as part of his children's primary school years.  The girls find some old school friends to sit with and share giggles and whispers with.

About 60 attendees are facing the front of the activity room in which they are gathered.  Only the guest speaker and the church minister are at the front, now. The church's pastor is very casually dressed, with Bermuda shorts, sandals and a shirt from the Pacific

Islands. Quickly picking up that the minister Neil Potts had invited the speaker after meeting him when on a missionary trip to Fiji.

When the guest speaker comes to the microphone, Michael immediately recognizes his face and sits there glued to his seat.

Good evening church. It is a pleasure to be here among you, and, for anybody who does not know, me my name is Karl Crawford. I will say a short prayer before I give my testimony, which by the power of the Holy Spirit, will touch and change lives tonight."

For nearly forty minutes Karl speaks with such passion and conviction that Michael and a few others are lost in time as they heard his story. Michael knew some of it from the stories that advertising consultants told him as office gossip. That Karl was the managing director and very successful licensed estate agent. Who suffered within two years losing his wife to breast cancer at age 46 and his eldest son in a fatal light plane accident while sightseeing over Fiji. That within 12 months he became a "Born Again" Christian. He sold his majority share in the estate agency and returned to Fiji. Took to teaching business skills and also gave away over 50% of his personal wealth.

What touches Michael is his ethos that you,
"Don't give away your inner peace and health to just gain something."
That Karl had discovered true peace and happiness by the blood of Jesus Christ. The minister is again up the front of the small congregation with the guest speaker Karl Crawford. They are there for the altar call. With passion and pleading not to hold back both men urged anyone, who did not know Jesus Christ as their personal savior to step forward and commit their lives to Jesus.

By the second altar call, Michael is overcome with conviction and goes up to the front of the common room, saying the sinner's prayer. Ms Casey calls out repeatedly "Praise God," and the girls look at each other, confused about what is happening to their dad.

It is late on Sunday night as Michael puts the rubbish bins out before going to bed. Placing the previously treasured pornographic magazines in the household bins and looking up at the night stars and closing his eyes as he feels the night air. Michael feels a weight somehow lifted off his shoulders. Now he is hoping he can be the husband and father, he needs to be.

"The man of change, for his life has changed." Karl Crawford had told him warmly embracing him and calling him, "Brother."

He explains this, to Connie who shakes her head and repeats again.

"I am and will always be a Catholic."

It is the first night he can fall asleep easily, not worried about money, kids and especially Connie.

*Chapter 10*

*THE CONFRONTATION*

It is now early May 1996.  Again Connie and Michael are having a meeting with Dr Bronwyn Heath in her office at Princess Margret's Reproductive Biology Clinic. It is a cold May morning and winter already is here.

"I am sorry but I will not do that."
Declares Michael which draws a sudden frown and angry stare from Connie.
"It is a matter of personal choice but I personally will not be using the facilities here or at any clinic in regards to IVF."
Rarely had a man objected to a semen analysis the way Michael had so Dr Heath explores alternatives.
"Michael you are aware that we, you guys, can't do direct intracytoplasmic sperm injection (ICSI) without your sperm, since you also now object to donor injection. So do you object on religious grounds or something?" With Connie looking away now furious, Michael carefully gives his answers to both of them.
"It is those rooms, plus I have to drive to Melbourne every single time, it's the time off work, even the cost of petrol plays into it.  I also can't masturbate anymore as a matter of personal faith."
Leaning back in her chair, Dr Heath quickly explores the options.
"I see. I see now your concern."
Laughing lightly to herself Dr Heath says,
"You are not the first man to object to the private room arrangements we have here.  It is unfortunate that we do not have the funding to upgrade the rooms.  You could drop your semen jar into the andrology laboratory at Frankston hospital.  They will test the sample and fax the results to us."

Looking at Connie, Dr Heath continues on with her explanation.

"You will still need to ejaculate into the jar, just do it during sexual intercourse."

Looking very tense and having trouble controlling her emotions.  Connie then asks,
"What day of my cycle would you like us to fuck?"
She is looking out the window, holding back her inner disgust at having sex with Michael, that way.

Without batting an eyelid Dr Heath continues, on.
"Michael, I will give you three andrology sperm analysis forms so you will not have to come here again for testing.  As for you, Connie, with now two stimulated cycles plus two donor semen direct injections which were unsuccessful.  It's time we had a good look at your uterus, ovaries and do a cervical evaluation.  Please see my office secretary to book the earliest dates available for the ultrasound and biopsy."
It will be another month before those results are available, for them to discuss with Connie's local doctor. The ultrasound showed a small ovarian cyst that needed further medical review and delay future treatment.

It is early in October 1996 and it is 12.30 on a weekday.  Michael and Connie have just come from the local gynecologist. They begin to argue as they walk into the family home.
"You told me that your endometriosis was not the cause of, not getting pregnant. You said it was me," raising his voice with rising anger.
"You said to your doctor that now you want it bloody investigated."
Not holding back as the children are at school and making his point.

39

"Now I find out that, between the three of you, that you have decided to take a treatment break and do further investigations on the both of us?"

"I was fine before trying IVF, now I am writing to them for answers and I never said you were the total cause."

"Do you realize what these treatments have cost us in time, money and it's stuffing up our kids' lives." Connie fires back, moving right up to Michael's face.

"If you had working balls in the first place, this would never have happened."

Now, a threat of her own finally comes out.

"You know how I feel, no kid, no marriage simple as that."

"Listen, have we the chance to build our own home early next year for the children who are with us now.  No shared bedrooms, our own home."

Knowing Connie's mind was firm and needing to go back to work with an unwinnable argument Michael leaves.

"You     can't     keep     saying     that     Connie." Knowing and fearing it could be true.

"Yes I can, no kid no marriage."

Michael leaves the conversation there and goes back to work, without eating lunch at home as he had planned.

Dinner in the family home and all five children are seated quietly at the table, so they do not upset mum/Connie who has been drinking since school pick up.  It is late November 1996, when Michael comes home at 6 pm and gets "the look" from all the kids and knows what to do. Slowly talking to all the kids, watching as Connie cooks dinner, Michael starts to take over the cooking from Connie.  This is fine by her as it lets her refill her glass and lean on the kitchen bench

Unsteadily. It is not long before Michael notices that she has been crying, sometime that afternoon.

Seeing the wide eyed look from Anna as Michael asks Connie,
"Are you OK, it looks like you have been crying?"

"Am I OK, am I OK? Well I received a phone call from Bronwyn who informed me, that the biopsy showed what she said again."
Clearly having some trouble remembering what was told to her.
"No evidence of endometriosis, hyperplesia or malignancy there."
Thinking quickly Michael responds,
"That's good news isn't' it?" immediately regretting saying that.

"What it means is that there is no way we are going ahead with buying the land and building next year. WE have to do ISCI."
She looks directly at Michael as if to challenge him to finish the conversation.
"If we don't-you know what that means."

*Chapter 11*

It is now the beginning of June 1997, having been on the Princess Margret's Reproductive Clinic's waiting list since prior to Christmas. Connie is to have an A.I. Cervical Evaluation and is sitting and reading a magazine, in the IVF waiting room.

"Boy is it a busy place here this morning." Connie says to one of the other IVF ladies, who have been trying for over two years like Connie to conceive.

"It sure is and most of them are regulars but there is a lady whom I have never seen before."

"My name is Candice Allen, by the way."

"Pleasure to meet you, I am Connie Reid." Connie is going to start asking questions but Birdie, one of the nurses, comes in looking around the waiting room, searching for Mr & Mrs Alimo.

Both Connie and Candice look curious as to why. Bridie sees Mrs Alimo by the water cooler.

"Mrs Alimo I have been looking for you. We are waiting for you."

Still looking around the waiting room Bridie asks,

"Where is your husband Mrs Alimo?"

In Broken English, Mrs Alimo replies,

"He is at his panel shop. Why, what do you want him for?"

With a mild cough Bridie answers.

"We can't start the treatment without his contribution."

Mrs Alimo has a surprised look on her face but all those who heard the conversation try to hide their laughter. Connie and Candice exchanged mobile phone numbers and become close friends that morning.

Connie and Michael are in their bedroom, it is 10 am on a Wednesday and Connie is lying on top on the bed covers, naked from the waist down. Michael is completely naked.

"Grab a towel from the bathroom cupboard in case you miss again."

"With you lying there rigid like that, there's is no chance I will miss."
"Don't think for a minute, I plan to enjoy any of this."
Connie remains lying on her back not listening; her mind elsewhere. Michael making sure he will withdraw his penis, just before the desire to ejaculate takes matters out of his hands.  For a woman in her late 30's Connie still has an attractive body. Establishing a controlled rhythm, so he could ejaculate at will, he hopes that Connie will have an orgasm but doubts it and today doesn't mind.  He is pleased with himself as he counted the squirts of his ejaculation.
"You know you look like you're really enjoying this."
"I will only enjoy holding our own baby when this is all over.  I know they pray for us at your church.  Louise Preston told me yesterday at school."
"Yeah, well ask the virgin mother and the pope for a miracle too."
"I doubt they would agree to any IVF.  The church says it's not natural."
"I can understand why."
Thinking this was all Michael could say, after what he has just performed.  Now they are going to Frankston to drop off the jar and go shopping.

It took them twice to ask directions before they found the Frankston Hospital's andrology laboratory which is around the rear of the hospital.  They are inside the building but not sure which area or counter to go to hand over the jar. Handling in the jar of semen, Michael approaches the counter after seeing a man with a green uniform standing near the collections sign.  With a confident greeting Michael introduces himself to the staff member at the counter and is somewhat surprised by his response.

"Well what have you got there?"

Taking a closer look, as he checks the details of the paperwork he remarks.

"I say, you have been busy this morning."

Adding one final remark.

"Good effort too."

Suddenly all of Michael's inner confidence vanishes as he realized that obviously the man was a smart arse. Connie also hears his manner of speech. This makes her cough. For Michael it suddenly brings back the frustration of his experiences with Alpha/Stork IVF and Princess Margret's private rooms. As they open the door to leave Michael whispered to Connie,

"Did you hear that guys comments and tone of voice?"

"Sure did."

"Smart arse or what."

"He sure is."

Connie and Michael are sitting down at a table in the food court area of Karingal Hub Shopping Center at Karingal. They are seated together and starting to eat their noodles when Louise Preston and her husband sit down next to them talking excitedly. Michael is seated closer to Louise and Robert Preston. He has hardly seen them both since their wedding day, he asks them,

"Why are you two newlyweds so excited?"

Without thinking Louise replies happily.

"Were pregnant, we just got the news."

Upon hearing that Connie spits out her tea a sudden emotional flush comes over her face as she realizes they have been married less than three months. The initial joy quickly vanishes; Louise puts her hand to her mouth as she sees the impact of the news on Connie's face.

"I am so sorry, I didn't mean to gloat or anything." An awful silence comes over the four of them and Connie gets up from the table and just walks away. Michael assesses the situation and reassures them both of their good news and that Connie will be fine.

It takes a frantic 20 minutes to find Connie who has been crying and go back to their car.  Connie comes down with a bad throat infection and the cycle was canceled later that month.

*Chapter 12*

It is a Saturday evening in late July 1997 Michael and Connie are alone in their bedroom.  It is 7 pm.

"Be careful.  Those needles hurt."

"I am being careful Connie.  It's not easy to get the exact spot, and I have never done this before.  How many needles do you need for this cycle?"

Very carefully Michael injects the needle at the top of her right buttocks in the area indicated by the nurse at Princess Margret's.  The clinic is hoping to stimulate Connie's ovaries to harvest up to four eggs for ISCI. All is going well.  Only two inseminated eggs will be placed using ISCI, to reduce the chances of multiple fetuses being conceived.

Pulling up her pants and turning to face Michael, Connie holds up three fingers and shows him the paperwork to indicate which days on her cycle he is to inject her.

"That one hurt by the way."

Was all she says before taking the syringe from his hand and leaving the room to dispose of the needle. Michael then leaves the bedroom to make a Milo and watch Carlton play Sydney on television. They hardly speak to each other again that night.

Michael left the newspaper in July to become a real estate consultant in Rosebud, where they live. It is now the middle of September.

In the back ground Connie is playing a song by Heart, "All I wanna do is make love to you." Michael feels the need to confront Connie while at home alone.

"Look, all of my pay from the newspaper since July has been spent paying bills and IVF, acupuncture visits which you have become obsessed about. Why do you keep playing this song?"

"You fucking cunt! That's all you crap on about, money, money, money. What about what I'm going through, you arsehole. You think I care about money, when I see that holier than thou Louise Parker walking around, showing off her baby bump!"

Without reason Connie explodes and spits at Michael and slaps his face. The instant physical response from Michael is to slap Connie across the face hard also. Shocked by what Michael has done, she tries to scratch his face. Michael quickly counters with a hard right fist twice, to the side of Connie's head which seriously hurts her as she drops to the floor clutching her face.

Feeling stunned and trying to figure out what just happened to them Michael kneels down next to Connie.

"Baby I am so sorry."

Connie pushes Michael away and stands up then looks at him crying in pain, giving him a warning.

"You ever hit me again like that and I promise I will stab you."

Michael picks up all the kids from school as Connie lies on the bed, her head throbbing from the assault. She does not go to work for two days hiding the black eyes. She also rings and cancels the cycle with Princess Margret's, informing them it was for "Personal reasons."

*Chapter 13*

It is the middle of October and Michael has driven with Connie to Princess Margret's to support his wife on day 11 of her menstrual cycle. This is the day that the two eggs are to be inserted and as Connie may suffer some discomfort. Michael is to drive Connie home and is waiting in a large common waiting room. He now understands the waiting game he can see around him. He notices the blue collar working man in his overalls, the business man in his dark suit. Next to him, nervously waiting is the Indian couple, also sitting patiently.

Michael counts close to 14 couples, all from different nationalities, all seeking to have a baby together. Whatever the reason for their infertility, he wants to let them know they are not alone, so he is not alone. He wants to reach out but knows he never will.

Since last month's home incident the girls have hardly spoken to him. Connie's family and children are becoming very outspoken and blaming Michael for not supporting Connie enough. Michael has avoided going to church on the Sunday nights but builds on the real estate listings from Karl Crawford. It is all he feels he can do.

Seeing the waiting room full of people somehow, he prays this ongoing bad dream will soon be over, never realizing how soon it would end.

## Chapter 14

It is now late November 1997 and Connie is again undergoing a direct injection using ISCI with two stored embryos.  The previous cycle in October did not result in conception of a pregnancy.  It is a Saturday night and everyone is at home with Michael watching "The Bill" on ABC television when all hell breaks loose.  Michael is seated in the lounge room enjoying television.  His wife's mood had worsened since taking a phone call after dinner from her friend Candice Allen. It is Anna who is now the target of Connie's wrath so Michael decides to listen in as Connie starts yelling at Anna.

"You little bitch."

Michael hears Connie hit Anna, so immediately he races into the kitchen dining area to confront Connie.

"What the hell are you doing? Leave her alone. What's the problem?"  Connie is furious and responds with, "She's lying at school about homework help to Louise Parker."

"What are you on about?" Michael is dumbfounded, by Connie's sudden changing behaviour.

"It's true.  She says that Julie gets help but not her. That's a lie."

Before Michael can respond she pushes Anna against the kitchen wall holding her, "If you ever."

Something inside snaps in Michael, so he forcefully pushes Connie away from Anna.

"Dad, get her away from me."

All five children are now in full view of the argument taking place. Rushing out of the bathroom where Sandra and Julie are brushing their teeth.

Connie turns her attention to Michael.

"I told you what would happen if you ever laid a finger on me again."

Now Michael speaks as a father, for the first time.

"I have not hit you but if you ever threaten Anna again like that, we will leave you."

Now all five children start yelling threats at their step parents and step brothers and sisters.  Total dysfunction and built up venom occurs, as Bobby goes rushing to his mother's side.

"I am going to bash you when I'm bigger; I'm telling my dad to bash you."
Michael now calls for calm and tells everyone in the room.

"No one is to touch anyone anymore, is that clear, listen all I want to do is watch television in peace."

After a short silence from everyone, peace is finally restored.

"Listen everyone.  Calm down.  Go to your rooms, please. No more arguing.  Settle down Connie."

Michael turns his back and walks out of the kitchen. Now in a total daze as to what has come over Connie, he walks towards the couch and is unaware of her coming up behind him.  Feeling a punch to his back, Michael spins around to see Connie with a kitchen knife in her hand.

"Did you just stab me?"
Connie blinks and shakes her head as the realization of what she has done hits her, collapsing on to the floor. Both Sandra and Anna come rushing into the lounge room to their father.

With screams from both girls towards Connie, both are filled with terror at seeing blood running down their fathers back. All Michael can think of is to yell at the girls to grab some clothes as he staggers to the bedroom to grab his wallet and car keys. The triage nurse at Rosebud hospital listens to his explanation that he cut his back falling off the garden shed.

Another emergency nurse just gives him a sideways look and says,

"Funny, over my years I seen a few blokes fall off the garden shed."

Bob and Carol are sitting quietly at home when they get the phone call from Michael that they are coming to stay for a while.

Michael makes it clear to his wife the next day, as he sits in his car.
"No more IVF Connie, no more."

She crosses her arms and looks away, tears in her eyes.
"Candice is starting her second trimester.  She told me last night."
"I'm happy for this Candice but I will not be doing IVF, final."
Then Michael starts his car and drives away without looking back.

*Chapter 15*

It is a Sunday in late February 1998, it is Bob's birthday and all available Reid family members are present except Michael's wife and her children. Forthright conversations are taking place between the family about Michael's marriage to Connie and the feelings of Sandra & Anna. It is a cloudy but sunny day with the BBQ birthday a family tradition.

"Listen mum, I agree with everything you said and I truly did not know that Bobby was also threatening the girls when I was not home. What am I to do? Yes Connie wants to reconcile and do IVF, and I would like to reconcile but not with IVF hang over us."

Carol makes her views known.
"That night you first came home to us, the girls were terrified by what they saw. Connie's not in a good state of mind and besides the girls want to leave."
"I know that mum, but that makes another marriage on the rocks. And me a two time loser." Michael sees outside on the veranda an outline of an unknown woman and children.
"Forget your pride and look after your daughters. You all deserve better."
As if the timing was planned Michael sees his sister Melissa arrives with a pretty lady who was accompanied by two school aged children whom he guesses must have been hers. The family gathering quickly moves outside to the garage beer fridge. Michael is reluctantly drinking the beer given to him by his dad. His sister Melissa waits to introduce the woman whom she brought to Bob's birthday gathering.
"Stop being a snob and let me introduce my friend to you."
His sister Melissa calls out from outside the garage.

Michael sees his mother looking on from the verandah. With confidence this lady friend walks up to Michael and offers her hand in a handshake, which he accepts.

"So you're Michael. Your sister has told me so much about you."

Upon hearing this, Michael panics at the thought of what this lady has been told. Seeing a startled look in his eyes she adds,

"Relax its' all good. My name is Tania by the way."

Hoping to end this conversations straight away Michael announces, blowing any matchmaking attempts by his mother and sister.

"Nice to meet you my name is Michael. I am twice married and I can't have any more children."

Tania gives Michael a smile.

"That's cool with me; I have my two children which I am happy with. I am not seeking to have any more." Knowing he just said something stupid, Michael excuses himself and goes to the fridge in the garage to grab another beer. Suddenly the urge to reconcile with Connie and the kids becomes a mixed emotion.

It is 10.20 am on a Wednesday morning in early March and Michael and Connie are meeting at the Jetty Road Cafe, sitting outside alone to talk reconciliation and moving back home permanently.

"Look it's been over 3 months now. When are you bringing the girls back to stay full time? No more of these trial sleepovers."

"It's not as easy as I hoped; they are against you being mum again."

Seeing the hurt in Connie's face Michael adds with perfect timing,

"Since seeing you put a knife in my back."

"Well I vomited all that night and hardly slept for a week after. I warned you not to hit me again."

Connie says this firmly through gritted teeth, looking away remembering the night it all fell apart.

"Connie, I did not hit you that night but I do acknowledge that I have hit you twice before. I was also cold and at times aggressive towards you."

Taking a sip of his coffee, while looking directly into Connie's eyes.

"All of this is since we started doing IVF. Which is I believe is harmful for OUR relationship, YOUR marriage and the children, ALL of us."

Michael strongly emphasizes those points. He has thought of it for days and how to say it to Connie.

"To me, as much as it is painful, I have realized that I am complete." Seeing the loss and startled look in Connie face he struggles on.

"I know that I will not have any more children. I've accepted this. I still want to be involved in a family but not that way."

Immediately on hearing this, tears swell up and start rolling down Connie's face and she does not try to wipe away or stop them.

"So you are asking me to give up trying to have a baby, for you. Because, now, you don't want a child with me. To me you're a complete arsehole."

Gathering her thoughts, Connie gives her own message.

"I will not give up this desire in wanting to have a baby, Michael."

"Connie, I'm asking you that we have at least a 12 month break from any treatment so we can put our lives back together."

"We have had a 3 month break as it is. I have written to Bronwyn and she phoned me. We can start again next month. Dr Heath said they will try different medications, as the last two cycles made me feel ill. Please, Michael."

Before she can speak further, Michael puts his hand up which grabs Connie's attention.

"I am sorry that is not happening. Something else you need to know, I have a lease option on a home.  If you insist on IVF, the girls and I will be moving out by the end of the month."
Taking the last sip of his coffee, Michael finishes what he has to say.

"We will not be doing IVF now Connie.  The price is too high. I will come and collect our stuff next week.  By then I will have spoken to the landlord and will sign over the house to you."

Standing up Michael ends the meeting.

"We need 12 months more for us to work all our issues through."

With that, Michael walks inside the cafe, pays for the coffees and leaves.

Connie sits there and starts crying again.  She sits there totally alone as she thinks of a way to make Michael come back to her.

### Chapter 16

Michael is seated with Bob & Carol in their dining room, having a coffee. It's late March 1998.

"The only thing that I'm funny about is that it has, like, painted pink walls in the bathroom.  Otherwise it's a great house. The girls love it as they have their own bedrooms each again."

"What are you going to do for washing and drying clothes?" asks Carol the practical grandparent.

"I will have to go to the laundromat until I get paid again in about 3 weeks. Otherwise with my original furniture and the beer fridge, we will be fine."

"We will stay away from coming to your house until you are settled in. I will give you some extra sheets and pillowcases I have, for times like these."

"Thanks mum, for everything. I know this has been difficult for you and dad, but the girls are really happy with my decision."

As an afterthought Carol mentions,

"Melissa has told me that Tania is now leaving her house in Somerville and moving to Rosebud."

"Why," asks Michael slightly upbeat at that thought.

"Wants to get away from her ex's family and make a fresh start plus be closer to Melissa and, um, you."

"Really?" is all Michael can say.


It is now a Wednesday afternoon in the second week in April and Michael is seated at the laundromat waiting for the dryers to finish.

"Hello, stranger. What are you doing here?"

Michael looks up from the magazine he is reading to see Tania and her children come in with a basketful of washing after school. Michael asks the same of Tania who informs him that.

"I am waiting for Nathan to come around one afternoon to hook up the washing machine to the taps."

She explains that there is a cap on the tap placed by the last tenant and she cannot remove it.

In part truthfulness and opportunity Michael states. "Knowing my brother-in-law, he could take a week to get around looking at it. I can do it this evening if you like."
Tania smiles and says,
"Your sister said you would probably say that. I accept your offer but it will cost you a coffee or a glass of wine."
An unpleasant memory jumps out at Michael.
"Coffee will be fine. What number did you move to again in Sixth Avenue?"
"Yes Sixth Avenue, number 144."
Michael asks "Will after dinner be, OK say, 7 pm?"
"That will be fine.
Michael's dryers have stopped. He empties them and says his goodbye.
Michael and Tania are seated at her coffee table in her home in Sixth Avenue. It is 7.25 that evening.
"If you don't mind me asking, did you take anything with you or have to start all over again?"
Tania politely asks.
"In truth 50/50 as some things were mine before and some things, Connie refused to have."
Explaining further Michael tells Tania that,
"I asked for a 12 month trial separation, months ago. Because of what my girls went through during IVF. Connie's one very, very determined woman." Now it was Michael's turn to ask a question.
"Why did this bloke Darren walk out on you?"
"He left me for another woman, who had no baggage, as he called it."
"Ouch, very hurtful," is all Michael can think to say, looking away.

"Yes it was at the time but I am over that now, which means if you would like to see me again, you must make your own choices.  Melissa told me to give you my home number.  Ring me when you know what you want."

With that understood Michael finished his coffee and said goodbye.

## Chapter 17

It is a Thursday night in late April and Michael has invited his immediate family to his new house's lounge room to celebrate Sandra's 14th birthday.  It is to be a quiet gathering, every member of the families who could make it, at Sandra's birthday gathering. To support and help Michael. He knows that they understand, the difficult time he was going through. The whole family gives Melissa a nod of the head when she comes in with Tania and her children. Michael makes himself busy making tea's and coffee, while Sandra opens presents and is told repeatedly how much she had grown.  It is only as everyone is preparing to leave by 9 pm as all the children still had school the next day that Tania approaches Michael who was doing some washing up.

"You have not called, after two weeks.  Does that mean you still want to reconcile with your wife?" Shaking the water from his hands then drying them Michael turns and faces Tania to answer her question,

"No I do not, as Connie still insists on doing IVF again.  I have even told her dad who dropped in I will not go through it again."

"Did you see how all the kids intermingled and were happy and laughing tonight? That's all I'm looking for in a relationship, relaxed and happy?"

"You know that helps my thinking heaps you saying that."

Before he could say anything more Tania finishes with.

"This should help even more, I am not going anywhere."

She gives him a peck on the cheek before saying goodbye.  Michael walks to the front door as the family leaves en masse.  Tania, as she is walking to Melissa's car, mouths to Michael, "Call Me."

Michael nods and, as he shuts the front door, his daughter Anna gives him a knowing look.

*Chapter 18*

With the girls now being 14 and 12 years old Michael feels it is safe to leave them at home and spend an evening with Tania talking and watching television at her lounge room in 6th Avenue.

"The girls are happy at home probably watching "Neighbours" and then "Friends," both shows I do not watch but please don't let my feelings stop you from watching what you like in your home."

"I am not a big watcher of television but Simone likes to watch Neighbours which is OK by me."

"Why isn't she watching television now?"

"Adam went off to his bedroom to play at 7 pm and Simone is still reading. She knows to turn off her bedroom light at 9.00 pm as she has school tomorrow. She told me she wants us to have time alone, also behave ourselves."

"Simone must know more than me," Michael half jokes, now a little bit unsure.

Sensing this, Tania offers him a Milo which he accepts and she excuses herself as the kettle boils away. Bored with what is on Michael changes the channel and watches a fishing documentary. He pulls his feet on the couch and curls up while the gas wall heater extrudes warmth as he relaxes and enjoys his evening. After a short time, Tania appears in a long nightie with slippers holding a Milo out for him.

"I hope you don't mind but I like to get ready for bed before watching television. I feel more comfortable like this."

"That's fine by me. It's your home."

Is all Michael could say as he racks his brain as to where this evening is leading.

"You look pretty settled in yourself, sitting there all curled up on my couch. I see you have already changed the channel on the television also."

She gives a grin as she hands him his Milo.

"Melissa told me that you are a television hog" and she gently prods him in the ribs.

"Hey watch out!  I nearly spilt Milo on your couch."

"Well hurry up and drink your Milo. There is something I want you to do."

Suddenly, confused looking around the lounge room.

'What do you want me to do?"

Tania responded dropping her gaze, "Kiss me, silly."

The fishing documentary is quickly forgotten as is his Milo. Slowly but surely Michael begins to feel more confident holding on to Tania and beginning to feel the warmth and smell of her skin. A million thoughts begin to swirl inside Michael's head as he holds Tania returning her passionate kisses. After feeling her breasts against his jumper, Tania moves asking Michael to take off his jumper.

"That's better." Michael has to ask about Simone and Adam being in the house.

"Will the kids be OK seeing me with you on the couch?"

Tania gives a slight laugh.

"I have said good night to them and told them if they stay in their rooms, they can buy some sweets from the school canteen tomorrow."

Michael takes a sip from his Milo and smiling asks Tania.

"Just what are you up too?"

"Well I am sitting on a couch next to you and I am hoping to have a good time."

"We are already, I think,"

Michael responds unsure of what to say.

"It will get better once you figure out one thing."

"What's that," confused again.
Moving closer to kiss him again Tania whispers,
    "I'm not wearing any underwear."

That is the first of many times they had sexual intercourse on that couch.

Tania asks later why Michael turned away and groaned loudly during his ejaculation. She is surprised when her new lover, informs her,
    "I have not ejaculated for well over 2 months since I was with Connie."
Michael explains to Tania he does not masturbate or anything else at all, because of the IVF tests.

### *Chapter 19*

Michael is sitting in his office at Crawford's & Associates Real Estate on a Friday afternoon in late May, planning the Open for Inspections he has that weekend. The receptionist puts through a call and walks down to his office to inform him that Karl Crawford is on the telephone for him. From his first hello, Michael immediately knew something was up. Firstly Karl asks about his listings and what Michael is doing. Then Karl moves to the reason for his call.

"Michael I must tell you that Neil's church service had an unexpected visitor two Sunday nights ago. I must say, from what Neil and Louise Preston told over the telephone was difficult to hear."

Having no idea as to why Karl has called about Michael responds,

"I am not sure as to what this has to do with me, Karl?"

"It was your wife Connie. She told Louise that you left her for another woman. Also that you were violent to her during the marriage."

Now Michael immediately understands when Anna said that Louise Preston did not wave to them when they drove past each other on Tuesday.

"Karl, I can assure you, what you were told is not totally correct."

"Sorry, Michael. It does not concern me as to who did what. The fact is you have a hurting wife. It is obvious that sin and separation from God's word have become factors in your marriage. To her eternal credit, Connie has recommitted her life to Christ and is asking the body of Christ to help put together her life and marriage."

Expecting what was coming next Michael bravely asks, "What would you like me to do Karl?"

"It's not up to me to tell any man what to do.  I myself have remarried and also know the challenges of a blended family.  Reading God's word daily and humbling ourselves before the cross works for my family.  What I can say is that you need to ring Neil and arrange some counseling sessions with your wife pronto."

"I must say that when I owned Crawford & Associates we made critical decisions, based on an agent's character and personal behaviors.
Now, I do not have a majority share in the company any more but you understand my word goes a long way in regards to listings, appointments plus recommendations. I am still a member of the REIV board, Michael. Since that time I meet you, business opportunities have flowed to your branch and yourself. I would be personally disappointed to not have it continue going forward. You understand my position, Michael don't you?  Let me know how your counseling goes."
He then hangs up.
Michael understands clearly and is not surprised to be called into his manager's office to explain what is going on.

It is Sunday evening at 6.45 and Michael is standing at the front door of Tania's home in Sixth Avenue.
"Melissa phoned me this morning. She told me your mother told her that you are going to marriage counseling with Connie on Tuesday night."
"Tania, let me come inside and explain.  It's not my doing."
"No, not tonight, as I am helping Simone with her school project then I am going to bed as I have my period too. I've have had a thumping headache all day." Michael can see from the body language and the tightly wrapped dressing gown that Tania was not in the mood to listen.

"I have also had Connie drive by this weekend with her children in the car and that Bobby is it, made a rude gesture to Adam who was playing in the front yard.  I don't know what games you are playing at but I have told Melissa too, you won't be coming back here, if you are seeing Connie."

"Tania, you are not hearing what I have told you on Friday night. I am being forced into it by Karl Crawford."

"Michael, I might be silly but I am not stupid.  No one could force you to do anything if you felt strongly enough about us."

Seeing genuine hurt in Tania face, Michael turns and steps away saying.

"Please don't think or say anything to anyone about us until I speak with you again."

Tania nods with tears in her eyes and says,

"I have to go help Simone."
Closing the door without saying goodbye.

*Chapter 20*

It is early June 1998, Michael, Connie, Pastor Neil Potts and Jill Coops, a Christian counselor are seated in the private boardroom in Frankston of Crawford & Associates. The time is 7 pm.

"Please pass on my thanks to Karl Crawford for the use of his private board room tonight."

Jill Coops firstly announces. Michael sits slouched in the chair and stares at the writing pad placed before him.

"As this meeting we all are searching for God's answers for this Christian couple with their pastor. Let us begin with a prayer first."

That is two things that surprises Michael that Connie is now a Christian and they are a couple. A heavy feeling comes over Michael.

Seated, Pastor Neil Potts bows his head and places open hands on the board table.

"Dear God, our heavenly father, the author and finisher of our faith, please may your Holy Spirit come into this room tonight, so that this Christian couple can retake their place within the body of Christ, with Jesus Christ at the head of the table. Amen."

After a silence, Jill Coops starts to explain and lay out the groundwork for the counseling session and the aims of that night's session. Jill speaks of "Hearing and Listening" to each other. Michael is caught off guard when he finds out that Connie has seen Jill twice before tonight, for personal counseling.

Feelings of sadness, regret and anger are bubbling below the surface for both of them. Michael struggles to hold it together and listens to Connie explaining what happened. That the love of her life, "Walked Out" on the marriage and started seeing another woman. That he "promised" to work on their relationship and marriage during the following twelve months.

Surprised he is able to speak at all without again yelling at Connie, Michael looks directly at all three of them first before speaking.

"I can see that how I respond to what Connie has said will begin or end how the night goes. It is true I had no real idea of the emotional, physical and financial cost of going on the IVF program. It is also true that we went into the system as a couple but came out individuals."

Taking a deep breath, Michael speaks from his heart.

"I am truly sorry for the hurt and the sense of loss that Connie is struggling with. The fact I have been confirmed as infertile and still unwilling must only compound any outcome regardless of doing IVF."

Jill leans forward and asks Michael,

"I am not sure of what you mean by regardless of doing IVF. Connie has agreed with me to wait 3 months before attempting conception with IVF again. Your wife is also willing to do a marriage rescue healing course run by Pastor Neil's church. She has openly admitted where she believes you both were let down by the clinics and the lessons learned from it. You must be reasonable and consider your part in the breakdown of the relationship, Michael."

Then her strong views become known.

"Do you think you can brush off your responsibility to your wife by having a new relationship with the first woman you meet?"

Knowing what is taking place, does not stop Michael from speaking for his first time with self determination and commitment.

"I am aware of the time and effort that you, Jill, and Pastor Neil are placing in being here tonight." Biting his lip, he looks directly at Connie.

"I am also aware of my personal failings and I do not blame Connie for every bad thing that happened during our marriage."

Connie's body language visually improves as she looks directly at Michael and she reaches for his hand which Michael accepted.

Not able to hold it in any more, Michael laments.

"I've lost count. I am not sure of how many injected eggs were implanted during those cycles but I can stand firm in saying they were all loved by me." Only now did they both grieve together. Tears have to be wiped away by the tissues given by Jill. After a short silence pastor Neil speaks quietly.

"The Lord knows them all Michael and I firmly believe their spirits are safely in the arms of Jesus. It was not lack of faith or anything like that on your behalf; it was simply medical science that did not work at that time."

Jill also speaks by informing Michael,

"No one, not even Connie is now blaming you for the unsuccessful pregnancies."

"That's not what she told me during those cycles," Michael said with his voice now raised, withdrawing his hand.

"What about her drinking and the names she called me? What about that?"

After looking at Neil, Jill confidently confirms.

"Connie now knows she said some wrong things, and has sought forgiveness for that. Your wife has also prayed with Neil and myself and we believe her when she said that she has forgiven you, too, for this current woman you are seeing."

Looking up from the table Michael looks at Jill and Pastor Neil speaking directly to Connie.

"I believe I am not in any relationship as of today, with this woman whose name is Tania by the way.

In truth I can say that Tania has placed no pressure on me, only accepted meas I am."
Jill Coops looks at Pastor Neil and asks Michael.

"Are you still seeing this lady, Tania?"

"I'm not sure," answers Michael who then looks at Connie.

"I believe that she told my sister she has backed right off and will not interfere in another woman's marriage."

Upon hearing this, Connie looks at Jill and smiles before asking Michael.

"Does this mean that you are not going to see this Tania anymore?"

"Probably not, Connie; probably not. Though I don't think I will come knocking on your front door soon."

After hearing that, Connie reaches for the whole box of tissues. Upon digesting his statement, Jill Coops speaks up.

"That's a hurtful thing to say, don't you think, Michael?"

"Again, probably is, but Connie now must understand that I will not be forced into going anywhere near an IVF clinic, ever again."

Then standing to indicate the session is finished.

"If Connie wants to have a marriage, that could be a possibility but if she wants a baby, Connie's on her own." Knowing he is finished with them all Michael speaks to Pastor Neil.

"I will be resigning my church membership as from tomorrow; you will get it in writing soon."

All Pastor Neil said was, "Accepted with sorrow."

"I thank you all for trying but sorry."

With that Michael knows that by Thursday he will have to resign or be dismissed from Crawford & Associates. It is then horrible feelings strike him being alone with no employment and unable to even pay his rent. His daughters deserve better and he knows it.

*Chapter 21*

Sitting in his car at the Rosebud Pier, Michael is tired from the little sleep he had the previous night. His pessimistic mood is deepened by the call from Brian, his old newspaper director. Michael is quickly disabused as to the possibility of returning to the Independent newspaper group. That that opportunity to return "anytime" was curtailed by the threat of losing thousands of dollars in real estate advertising from Crawford & Associates. Karl must have anticipated this, shutting down that little escape plan. Apart from the call on his mobile from Bob his father, Michael decides to drive to the pier and sit in his car, be anywhere but home. Then his mobile rings again and Michael answers it before looking.

"Hello, Michael Reid."

It is an unfamiliar voice on the other end. Michael struggles for a moment, trying to recognize the voice.

"Michael, its Ronnie C Long, calling. How is Rosebud pier this morning?"

Even though being caught off guard by Ronnie calling him, Michael comments.

"Miserable and cold. Just like how I am feeling. What gives you the joy of calling me again, Ronnie?"

"Well three things to be truthful. Firstly you should have known that Brian would say no to you." Michael's Jaw drops as Ronnie continues on, knowing he has him.

"Secondly, I hear that Karl will be coming to pay you a visit tomorrow morning at 9.30. You will get your marching orders. Thirdly I would like to interview you today about a sales opportunity with us at Long Real Estate. I am free right now."

It is Friday evening at Michael's home and Tania has been dropped off by Melissa his sister who is taking

Sandra, Anna, Simone and Adam to a kid's film at the cinema and McDonald's later on.

"You must tell me what happened on Wednesday. Who is this Ronnie Long? Your mum rang me and told me everything that happened."

Taking a sip from his Milo, Michael lets out a laugh and is smiling as he explains to Tania.

"Out of the blue I get this call from Ronnie, when I was at the pier. I was down there, thinking, as I knew I was in deep shit with Karl. Ronnie calls me and tells me he knew what was going down.

Later on he told me that receptionist girl at Frankston was his insider source. She had been since he sold her grandparents' home for next to no commission. That Ronnie is one sure smart operator. He also said that I could work every second weekend as well, keeping Wednesday as my day off each week."

Looking up from his Milo, Michael asks Tania.

"I have two week before I start my new job, will you come to Halls Gap with me?"

"I can't afford it."

"Ronnie has a mate who runs the Halls Gap caravan park and because it's winter, two hundred for 3 night's accommodation."

"Are the children welcome too?" Tania is unsure of the reason for the weekend getaway.

"Yes, we are all going away. The only hard part will be squeezing the four of them in the back seat of the Magna. Listen, sweetie, you are the one I do want to be with from now on. I am sorry for what has happened this last week."

Moving to hold her Michael reaches to kiss Tania who rises holding his hand and indicates she wants to go to the bedroom.

As Michael happily walks to his bedroom to make love he hopes the movie does not finish too early.

It is now early December on a Saturday morning. Michael is in the rear yard of a house in McCrae anxiously waiting on two phone calls.  One is from the vendors of the property, he has an offer on.  The other important call is from Tania who has gone to the doctors with Melissa. "Bloody mobile phones!" he thinks.
"People have them but they always seem to be out of range or turned off when you want them."
He nervously waits, while the potential buyers walk around the back yard.  Talking to each other and deciding how and where they could change things.  He has left two messages with the owners of the McCrae property and is hoping for a call back soon. Mentally agreeing that any and all offers should be put on paper, it shows "commitment" as Ronnie calls it.  The offer is still twenty thousand away from the asking price. Michael knows he had to start and negotiate with the potential purchasers down from Melbourne. It was then his mobile rings and he answers it without checking the number.
"Good Morning. Michael Reid speaking."
It was the voice he heard every day speak.
"Hello daddy."
Gulping to catch his breath, Michael responds,
"What? Oh my god."
"You are going to be a daddy, I am six weeks pregnant and it's for real."
As he takes in this unexpected news Michael is approached by his clients who want to talk to him.  All he could think of is to tell Tania,
"I have to go, love you and will speak to you later."
Only when Michael is back in his car driving to the office to sign up the offer with the clients he says out loud.
"How am I to tell my mother, Anna, Sandra and, holy shit; Connie?"

*Chapter 22*

*THE RESOLUTION*

It is in the end of January 1999. Michael is at home on his bed. It is 11 am and Michael is about to make 2 important phone calls. He is thinking it might be best to ring Dr Heath, on how he could break the pregnancy news to his wife. Michael dials the telephone number and it takes a couple of minutes of waiting before he is put through.

"Hello, Michael. How are you? It must be since early last year since I spoke with you. How is Connie? I have not spoken with her since late November." Immediately Michael is suspicious and corrects Dr Heath.

"Well, it was November 1997 when I last spoke with you, but, may I ask, why did you speak with Connie in November last year?"

"That was when she had the last of the ICSI transfer of two inseminated embryos which, unfortunately you're aware were unsuccessful."

"Excuse me' but did you say that Connie did ICSI last year?"

By now Dr Heath has picked up something is wrong.

"Yes Michael, 3 times I think, what's the issue with ICSI now? What is the nature of this telephone call today, Michael?"

"Please do not do any IVF or ICSI with Connie anymore. I withdraw my consent and permission, because we separated in March last year."

He senses the shock from Dr Heath and continues. "Not only that I have a new partner and she has completed her first trimester with our baby. My partner is 3 months pregnant. How could this happen? Since you said repeatedly, I was medically infertile."

Upon hearing this, Dr Heath finishes the conversation immediately.

"I am sorry but I will not be able to speak with you now anymore."

The telephone call ends there and then.

Michael is now holding the phone but not believing also what he has been told. It is then he realizes that a telephone call would not do. He would confront Connie tonight after she gets home from work. Feeling overwhelmed by everything, Michael just lies on his bed, feeling stunned by this news.

It is 7.30 pm and Michael has parked his car in Connie's driveway and is waiting for Connie to come out so he can confront her.

"Julie said you were parked in the driveway. Why are you here?"

Connie is about 10 feet away when she says this. Michael could see that she was tense and looks tired.

"Well, the truth is I had no intention of coming here but today's events force me too."

"What events are you talking about Michael? What are you on about? If you have come to have an argument or to threaten me, you can leave my property now."

"No I have not come to argue but, today, I spoke with Dr Heath and know about you doing ICSI last year. Just what the fuck were you up too?"

Immediately on hearing this Connie drops eye contact, turns and starts to walk back to the front door.

On seeing this Michael calls out.

"One last thing Connie. Stay right away from all of us and don't drive past Tania's home. She is 3 months pregnant with my child."

Immediately after hearing this, Connie stops as she doubles over at the front step. Michael, with some satisfaction adds one final threat.

"Looks like your insane plan is finished. Stay away from us or else."

With the neighbor across the road watching as he washes his truck, Michael backs out of the driveway and drives away.  Connie goes inside and collapses onto her bed and is inconsolable for an hour.

*Chapter 23*

It is now 9 pm on the 19th of April 2001 and Michael has finished writing his letter which he intends to read to Tania who is seated next to Michael and two weeks away from giving birth to their second son.

"You are going to make more enemies, by sending the letter."

"That is true but since you were pregnant with Andrew, it must be at least a dozen people who we no longer speak too. Especially many of the mutual church friends of Connie and me, but that is often the price you pay, when couple's split. You know that regardless of what Connie has done or said, I still believe what happened to us both was unfair.  This is my third and last attempt in writing this letter to the Infertility Treatment Authority, so here we go; I will skip the introduction.

I had a partially successful reversal performed by Dr Staffon in 1994. After the micro surgery, Dr Staffon told me he was able to rejoin the right side but it was not possible on the left. Testing in February 1995 confirmed the reversal was successful with a positive semen count present. We were referred to Alpha/Stork IVF clinic in our short discussion with Dr Ivan Sloob outlined a IVF program using ICSI (Intra Cytoplasmic Sperm Inoculation) due to high concentration of IgG sperm antibodies, in both the head and tail of the sperm.  In our brief discussion with Dr Sloob we only talked about the cost per cycle (approximately $1,400.00). Dr Sloob explained that the SMET testing showed that if we chose IVF, ICSI was our only option to achieve a pregnancy. Dr Sloob bluntly told us that my semen (sperm) is no good. Truthfully we were not comfortable with Dr Sloob's manner as we felt they were more interested in how many cycles we could afford with Alpha/Stork IVF.  We did pay the joining fees and have consultations with them but the cost per cycle was unaffordable to us at that time. We decided to transfer to the public health IVF clinic due to the cost savings and the initial manner in which they addressed our concerns."

Taking a sip from his coffee Michael continues reading the letter. "During our many discussions with Dr Bronwyn Heath, Senior register of the Reproductive Biology Unit of the Princess Margret's Hospital. She said her medical opinion which she stated verbally to both Connie and I, it was the presence of anti-sperm antibodies was the reason for our inability to achieve a pregnancy. We were never told that I was sub-fertile, only that I was infertile and the medical file has it listed as MALE INFERTILITY. The semen tests stated in 1995 when the Reproductive Biology Unit performed semen analysis for sperm mobility with one further test showing borderline penetration with donor mucus.

The tests performed on 16/11/1995, 30/9/96, 10/10/96, 31/10/96 and 17/1/97 were not using Worlds Best Practice. Instead of investigating the 10 to 12 factors that make up a complete semen analysis, all the focus was on my proven infertility from the earlier test results.

We were told repeatedly that Connie was not the problem as she had 3 children from her earlier marriage. At our insistence Connie had a laparoscopy and, as Connie recovered from the surgery Dr Heath told her that her tubes were blocked. Connie had a further test being a H.S.G, a dye x-ray of tubal patency. This test result was clear. No recorded explanation was given for the mixed results. The Princess Margret's Hospital never did a mucus test using my sperm and Connie's mucus to check for compatibility. It was during the years 1996 and 1997, that both of us asked a lot of medical questions the medical staff and were repeatedly left in no doubt that donor sperm or ICSI, were the only options open to us. It was during a cycle that we separated with the stress of the treatment pushing both of us beyond our breaking points. Connie had advised the clinic that she had bad reactions and side effects to the needles and fertility stimulants she was taking."

Michael smiles as he tries to explain his letter to Tania.

"This is where you come in. Shortly after we separated, I meet my current wife Tania Reid. I did inform her early in our relationship that I could not father any more children as I was infertile. Within six months of starting a consensual sexual relationship, I was in shock when she confirmed the pregnancy in early December 1998. In January 1999, I rang Dr Heath and informed her of my fathering a child when I was considered infertile by the clinic. Dr Heath denied this and informed me that she could not speak to me any further. After all the heartbreak that we went through it was very difficult to inform my then wife Connie. After our baby was born (Andrew James Reid 28/07/1999), I underwent further tests for Seminal Fluid examination for Infertility which showed no abnormality in the specimen (Copy attached). With me, receiving written expert advice from Dr Donald Carter F.R.A.C. S. F.A.C.S, I was never at any stage during 1995, 1996 and 1997 infertile." Taking a deep breath and sipping the last of his coffee.

"That the reproductive biology units of both the Alpha/Stork and Princess Margret's Hospital used highly speculative testing for infertility. That the presence of sperm antibodies appears to have been non-specific and not absolute. That I was able to achieve a pregnancy with another partner within a short period of time after separating from my ex-wife Connie proves earlier analysis to be flawed and misleading. To this day, Connie still suffers medically from being on the IVF program. Connie believes that the Princess Margaret Hospital was negligent with the treatment we received.

We both believe that mistakes were made and with no acknowledgment of the life changing consequences as a result of the experience during IVF.  It was during those years that I suffered from repeat episodes of throat and chest infections requiring multiple scripts of antibiotics until I had a tonsillectomy in 1997."

"At the times of the testing that I was on medication. I informed the clinics and it was recorded so. With the known and recorded side effects of antibiotics (Amoxycillin, copy attached), we asked if could be a possible reason for the poor semen results.  Having read through Connie's and my IVF medical file, at no point does it leave the reader in any doubt about my stated infertility.  The records show no other medical alternative treatment offered except IVF to achieve a pregnancy. When we asked for less intrusive and costly treatments we were told that IVF using GIFT and ICSI were our only hope. We investigated the possible usage of a course of quarter zone steroids to act against the sperm antibodies present but decided against it, as it could be harmful to my already weak immune system."

"This is where I get to the main points, hope it sounds alright. I am seeking a complete examination conducted by the Infertility Treatment Authority to investigate the facts as we believe them. That two approved IVF clinics failed in their duty of care towards my former wife and I. The tests performed were subjective at best and conjectural whether it was only the combined stress of IVF treatment and being on antibiotics factoring as the main reasons for a non pregnancy. The reproductive biology clinics did not use Worlds Best Practice, in the testing of seminal fluid infertility. These clinics were negligent in the scientific analysis they recorded in the medical file. That I was never "infertile" as infertility is

only a relative diagnosis with the parameters varying from clinic to clinic and the testing scientist from each other, as confirmed by Dr Donald Carter, Urologist. What is still unclear to us is the business relationship between the testing clinics and the referring medical specialists. That both clinics, directed
the treatment towards IVF when it was against our best interests."

"The medical actions need to be explained in detail as I have two naturally conceived pregnancies, I have achieved with another partner. Our second child is due on 01/05/01.   In conclusion I am seeking to appear before the Licensing and Approval committee for Infertility.  That I am asking to seek a response from Alpha/Stork IVF Private Hospital Pty Ltd and the Princess Margret's Health Care Network.   I also wish to appear in camera before the licensing committee to ask questions and be cross examined by the clinics medical directors and staff. All the findings of the committee be put on public record with any recommendations made, based on the committee's own findings. That we are seeking financial redress by mediation to bring this matter to a conclusion.  I also ask that this letter not be sent to the clinics and medical practitioners but only quoted from directly.  This matter confidential and I wish to be informed in writing, in a timely manner, as to what stage of the action process this matter has reached. Thank you for your understanding.

Yours sincerely, Michael J Reid."

"What do you think sweetie?  Think they will respond this time?"

Tania moves and gives Michael a kiss on the head and stands up showing her at nearly full term.

"Probably ignore you like the Medical Practitioners Board has. I am going to bed as your baby son is kicking me a lot while sitting there."

It is the 28<sup>th</sup> of April and Michael is with Tania sitting in a table in a food shop in the K-Mart Plaza.

Connie approaches holding a paper bag.
"Thanks for meeting us here, please take a seat."

"No thank you."
Connie replies standing looking very uncomfortable.
"I have Julie and Jason walking around somewhere looking for a couple of mother's day presents."
"Ok then.  I have received a letter of reply from the Infertility Treatment Authority saying that they have referred my complaint, to the Licensing Committee of the Authority for their consideration."
Now, looking again at the letter, reading out loud.
"It says they will contact me after they have met and they also ask have I forwarded the complaint to the Medical Practitioners Board."
"They are a toothless tiger; what they suggested was counseling between us."
Connie said this knowing how useless that would be.
"Well I will leave any settlement offers on my behalf with you.  I went through my personal things, the other day and found these."
Connie reaches in and pulls out three baby suits in three different colors.
"You are having a boy again are you?"
"Yes he's coming out on the 1<sup>st</sup>" Tania responds.
"A very active baby he has been kicking me while were sitting here."
"My Bobby was like that, he was ready to come out at 36 weeks.  Look, I have to go. Good luck with the baby," suddenly ending the conversation.
Connie hands the baby suits to Tania and leaves the cafe.
Michael watches Connie go and sees her wipe her eyes when she thinks she is out of sight.

*Chapter 24*

It is 10.30 am Monday 20th of May and Emeritus Professor Harvey Barton AO is seated with Bonnie Stewart the CEO of the Infertility Treatment Authority.

"You know I have said it often for some time now, the clinics needed to change the parameters of their methodology in their testing standards. What part of this letter from Mr Reid is a concern to you Bonnie?"

"The paragraph in which Mr Reid asks to appear in person, before the licensing committee. When it was drafted in 1995, the legislation, did not rule in or out an individual or a non legal entity challenging part or seek conciliation on the licensing conditions on a clinic."

Picking up the *Infertility Treatment Act* 1995, Bonnie continues.

"I'm just not 100% sure the administrative appeals tribunal would knock out any future application."

"Then we need to get in touch with the government solicitors office and receive expert advice before getting back to Mr Reid."

Shaking his head as Professor Barton rereads the letter.

"What about our friends at the two clinics involved?" Confusion from Alpha/Stork, also questions from the senior register at the Princess Margret's health care network. As requested board members will be here this afternoon at 4pm in the boardroom."

Bonnie informs the chairman.

"Good, I think you'd better order some refreshments as I believe the board has a lot to discuss and decide upon. From the quality and length of this complaint, we'd better make sure the authority is protected as a third party in any possible litigation. The minister's office has asked for a briefing paper for the health minister."

"Was it necessary to inform the minister this early on?" Bonnie asks.

"Very much so.  He apparently already knew about Mr Reid's complaints" was the final comment from Professor Barton.

The time now is 6.10 pm and the Infertility Treatment Authority Board is about to finish its response into the complaint received from Mr Michael Reid.

"Before we break for some refreshments, Bonnie will soon read what we recommend to the board what to do, with Mr Reid's letter of complaint and why.  Board members are fully aware that we have a new labor Victorian government and a Federal Liberal government seeking another re-election later this year." Now, having the firm attention of all present, Chairperson Professor Barton continues.

"It is of concern to Bonnie and the executive chair, that the Infertility Treatment Authority could be dragged into political commentary about Victorian clinic testing standards.  With a Full Court of the High Court case in September with single women's rights to access Victorian clinics, politics do come into play."
Now it was Ms Stewart's turn to speak to the board.

"It is on this basis that we are pleased with the board's approval to appoint Professor Harry Pollard as a specialist consultant to the Authority. Professor Pollard's initial tasks will be to undertake an audit of licensed places. To determine any impact of the treatment of Mr & Mrs Reid and single women as defined by the Infertility Treatment Act.  Professor Pollard's audits will conducted by the end of 2001.  The Authority is seeking to revise its own guidelines because of the changed understanding of the Infertility Treatment Act of 1995."

After two questions from board members the motion was passed by all present. Then Professor Barton then outlines his intended response to Mr Reid, before having his only malted scotch for the evening.

It is the 27th of May and Michael is reading the letter he has received from the Infertility Treatment Authority before dinner is ready.

"Dear Mr Reid, the Authority has reviewed your complaint and the Authority is required to satisfy itself that the Infertility Treatment Act 1995 contains provisions which empower the Authority to address this complaint."

"What does that mean?"
Ignoring the question, he reads on.

"To this end I wish to advise that the Authority is seeking further information, about those matters which pertain directly to the conditions of license.  Which have been granted to the Princess Margret Health Care Network and Alpha/Stork IVF Pty Ltd. These are the two places that provided the services with the approval of doctors, scientists and counselors and were responsible for your treatment.  It is the Authority's view that nearly all of the matters in your complaint should be directed to the appropriate complaints handling bodies. This may be the Health Services Commissioner or the Medical Practitioners Board."

Taking a deep breath Michael continues reading aloud as Tania places his newest son Lewis who is happily sleeping on his lap.

"You specifically requested an opportunity to appear before the licensing committee to review the licenses and approvals granted by the Authority.  The Authority does not have any specific powers which permit it to call approved practitioners to a meeting to respond directly to a complaint from a patient.  The ability to provide mediation and compensation rests with the Health Services Commissioner and should you wish to review a decision made by the Authority to grant a license or approval, this may be done through the appropriate administrative review processes. I have attached an extract of the Act containing these provisions.  I will write to you again once the Authority has considered the replies it will receive from the Princess Margret's Health Care Network and Alpha/Stork IVF Pty Ltd. Yours sincerely, Emeritus Professor Harvey Barton AO."

Looking down at his sleeping son, Michael looks up at Tania and says, "Looks like I will have to print the details again, photocopy the test results and post it to the Health Services Commissioner too."

"When will this all end," Tania asks as dinner is nearing being served.

"I don't know but we all deserve an apology and our money back.  I will write to them as soon as I can. What's for dinner sweetie?"

"Your favorite; curried sausages, with a pudding for dessert."

"Very nice."

It is the 12th of July and Michael is again reading to Tania his response letter to Ms H. Ryder who is the Health Services Commissioner for Victoria.  "Dear Helen, I am writing to you in response to the letter dated 29th of June 2001, from Professor David Clark Obstetrics /Gynecology Medico-legal Officer of the Hospital Support Unit of Princess Margret's Hospital."  Looking again at the letter Michael is hoping his spell check is correct. "In response to what was written, I would like to make the following comments to Professor Clark's letter.

"In regards to the presence of sperm antibodies, my former wife and I were told that the sperm antibodies were of IgG type and were present in 80 to 100% of Seminal Fluid examinations. These tests were conducted by the andrology laboratory of The Princess Margret's Hospital.  And stated that the sperm antibodies were the sole proven reason for the infertility as a couple. This was confirmed to us in writing by Bronwyn Heath MBBS, FRACOG Senior Registrar of the Reproductive Biology Unit on 2nd March 1998."

Now are you going to answer this time, Michael wondered? "Was I actually infertile?  We were told repeatedly that I was infertile by the medical staff concerned as it is clearly recorded- 31/10/1996 as MALE INFERTILTY? We always knew that I was not sterile because they were able to use my sperm to do ICSI
(Intra Cytoplasmic Sperm Inoculation). I was never classified as sub-fertile; in fact those words were never confirmed to us in spoken form or writing.  It is recorded from seminal fluid tests dated 16/11/1195 from the andrology laboratory of Alpha/Stork IVF and the comments are as read.  "On the basis of this analysis this patient is suitable for ICSI only."
"This is what we were told repeatedly throughout our Infertility treatment at the Princess Margret's Hospital during the years 1996, 1997 & 1998."
"Events have obviously proven this erroneous as I fathered two children by natural sexual intercourse.  I was never infertile as confirmed by Dr Donald Carter, Urologist. A examiner in Urology Royal Australasian College of Surgeons 1998-2000, also holder of the *Louis Barnett Medal* of the RACS in 1999, for outstanding contributions to Education Training and Advancement in Surgery."
Getting up from the table to turn the kettle on Michael continues talking.
"My former wife and I did go through cycles using IVF, ISCI and even donor sperm.  This does in no way mean that Connie was infertile that was not defined. Being close to 80% of couples not experiencing success using IVF treatment does not equate to ongoing infertility. We were not aware that sperm antibodies can go away slowly in men who have a vasectomy reversal over time. This being true, we ask what percentage does it occur and any current research to confirm this?  We were told that they would not go away naturally. This was the reason the usage of high dose cortico-steroid

therapy was recommended. What was not addressed in Professor Clark's letter was that the tests performed were indeed, world's best practice as recognized by The Infertility Treatment Authority.  The ranges for seminal fluid tests undertaken by Alpha/Stork IVF and the Princess Margret's Hospital differed from other independent clinics.  The accepted ranges were different for abnormal forms, velocity, motility and morphology. How can Professor Clark ignore Dr Donald Carter's belief that, results of semen analysis can vary from laboratory to laboratory. That indeed interpretation of both motility and sperm morphology is somewhat subjective."

"Like a lot of couples who were seeking help to conceive a child we did as we were told by the medical specialists involved.  We were ill-informed and that I was the problem as to why a child was not conceived.  We understand that some things can go wrong, from collecting the semen samples to Connie suffering severe side effects to some medications.  I will always hold the IVF experience for the marriage failing and the physical, emotional and spiritual breakdowns as well.  This is a burden I will always carry inside of me."
Looking at Tania, Michael asks,

"You ok with that?"

"It sounds a bit mushy, coming from you."

"I needed to put it in writing, even though I no longer feel that way. Anyway I will continue.  As I have earlier stated the cost of the IVF treatments is over $25,000.00 which does not include time off work, travel and medicine costs.  I have written advice as to seeking a court settlement, which could be 10 times the amount spent on treatment. I hereby give Professor David Clark consent to view Connie Ward's, (nee' Reid) medical file. (I have attached letter of consent from Connie Ward). I am also asking the Health Services Commissioner to arrange a meeting between the parties to negotiate a confidential satisfactory settlement.

Please confirm to me in writing that this information has been passed on.

Yours faithfully. Michael Reid."

It is the evening of the 26th of July 2001.  Michael is in a very happy mood and is excited as he rereads a letter from the Health Services Commissioner that arrived in the mail.

"Tania, listen to this. The Health Services Commissioner, Helen Ryder has accepted my complaints and decided pursuant to s19 (10) of the *Health Services (Conciliation and Review) Act 1997(the Act) to refer it to conciliation.*"

"Under the Act, a conciliator impartially encourages prompt settlement of complaints, a service to both parties, by arranging informal, confidential and privileged discussions between them.  Being available to assist in those discussions and helping them reach an agreement.   It goes on to say that everything is confidential and I am welcome to provide more information with my submission.  It is on the conciliation waiting list and a conciliator will be appointed to begin the conciliation process it's signed by the Chief Conciliator herself."

"So this is not over yet?"  Tania said frowning as she folded washing.

"No, but at least I will get some answers to my letters and they can't ignore me anymore, I hope."  Feeling some relief that he can see light at the end of the tunnel, Michael goes over to his youngest son who is lying in his bouncer.

"Both clinics will be spitting chips, about the Health Services Commissioner granting conciliation."

"It's like I said at the beginning, you are going to make more enemies."

"I think I already have."

Michael is again reading a letter sent by the Health Services Commissioner, in the bedroom of their rented home in West Rosebud.

He is speaking with the conciliator Julie-Marie Baldwin who is handling Michael's case.

"Well it's been nearly a year on the conciliation waiting list and I have written numerous letters with questions to the Infertility Treatment Authority and the HSC with few satisfactory replies."

"Unfortunately, Michael, your type of detailed complaints relies on two hospitals and a government appointed authority responding within their own particular time frame. I can see in your file copies of letters from your local and federal members of parliament about your medical complaints which have been forwarded to me regarding the time factor," Julie comments.

"Yes I have. So what now?"
Michael asks waiting to hear some positive news.

"It is exactly like I have written Michael. All going well we should be able to start conciliation in the next couple of months," Julie-Marie confirms.

"That sounds better but do you think the process will be finished by Christmas? I am asking that because we are thinking of buying a block of land at Glenrowan, and moving up there at the end of the year."

He smiles as Tania walks into their bedroom.

"Well, unless the clinics do not want to conciliate it should hopefully be finalized, usually within the next couple of months."

"That's great. Thank you very much for answering my questions."

"That's fine, Michael. I will write to you shortly with a date on which both clinics and the Infertility Treatment Authority will start the conciliation process."

"That's fantastic thank you."
Jumping on their bed which annoys Tania.

*Chapter 25*

It is the 18th of July and a meeting is being held at the offices of the Health Services Commissioner at 570 Bourke Street Melbourne.  Present are Michael Reid, Julie-Marie Baldwin and Ken Jackson for the Health Services Commission.  Present are the Medical legal officers for the Princess Margaret and Alpha/Stork IVF hospitals.  Also present is Danni Schmidt and Robin Marks from Conner/Coop & Co, legal defense lawyers for the IVF clinics.  After the somewhat tense and formal greetings are exchanged it is Ken Jackson from the Health Services Commission who laid out the ground rules for conciliation.  Everyone hears the words "no admissions or acceptance of fault, can be used in any court due to confidentiality clauses by any party."

When asked by Ken Jackson if there are any questions Michael quickly raised his hand.

"Where are the treating doctors to answer my questions?"

It was Professor David Clark, the obstetrics & gynecology medico-legal officer for the Princess Margret's Health Care network who answers.

"At this meeting they are not required to attend so myself and Dr Colin Barnes from Alpha/Stork IVF are here to answer your concerns.  We both have read the medical notes and your letters to the clinics."

With that, Ken Jackson calls the meeting to order and outlines the complaints from Michael Reid with the Support of Connie (nee Reld) Ward. Being the party who is seeking conciliation.  Michael is asked first to make his opening statement and ask questions but is told that the medico-legal doctors did not have to answer them.

Following on from the nod that Michael receives from Julie-Marie, he asks his first question.

"Who got the diagnosis wrong?  The clinics or us?"

It was Professor David Clark who answers first, confident of his reply.

"I will say that no one got it wrong because you were treated for infertility as a couple."
This brings an instant response from Michael.
"That's news to me. What about the letter from Dr Heath and all the tests that said I was infertile?" Addressing Michael like one of his first year medical students, Professor Clark corrects Michael.
"That is a relative term as you were predominantly infertile but, if one is being absolutely correct, it should be called sub-fertility problem."

"That also is news to me. I have never heard that before!" Michael looks at Julie-Marie who seems to be uncomfortable by the dismissive tone and body language of Professor Clark.
"Even a first year medical student would know that after a vasectomy reversal that sperm antibody levels fall over time, the same as any vaccinations also decline over time."
This time Michael jumps in speaking quickly.
"If that is so, then why did both hospitals andrology clinics say that ICSI or donor sperm was the only option? And were those testing standards worlds best practice? Why does Dr Donald Carter, a well known urologist say otherwise?"

"This Dr Carter is not an infertility specialist so his saying that, I dismiss straight away. He would not have the expertise or experience the World Health Organization scientists who work at our clinic have. Also the fact you have questioned testing standards I find disturbing as all standards were worlds best practice at the time and approved by the World Health Organization and other bodies."

At this point Ken Jackson of the Health Services Commission tries to regain focus of the discussion, so far.  He asks Michael if the responses given so far by Professor Clark answered Michael's questions about their IVF treatment.  Ken Jackson asks if Michael has one final question for Professor Clark to consider answering. Leaning forward, Michael, after looking at Julie-Marie, asks.

"How come the Infertility Treatment Authority allows specialists to be part owners of IVF clinics and the testing laboratories? Is this not a conflict of interest?"

One can see Professor Clark's nostrils flare as he stated firmly.

"Regardless of clinics proprietorship and that of the labs, we IVF specialists maintain the highest ethics. If you want to know about what the Infertility Treatment Authority decided you should ask them."

After Professor Clark answered, Robin Marks, one the lawyers closes his notebook on the table as an indication that the meeting is over. This catches the conciliators by surprise.

"Enough, we will not talk with Mr Reid any more.  We are done."

Michael looks intensely at Professor Clark before answering,

"No we are not."

Michael now realizes that the clinics are unaware that he was taking the Infertility Treatment Authority to the Civil and Administrative Tribunal at the end of the month. Julie-Marie, his conciliator, indicates for Michael not to leave straight away as she has something she wanted to tell him.  As the lawyers were leaving, Julie-Marie said to Michael,

"See that lawyer Robin Marks from Conner Coop & Co?"

"Yes, what about him?"  Michael responds.

"His firm, apart from defending medical lawsuits, has a long association in defending sexual abuse claims against victims by members of the Catholic Church."

"This means this is as far as any further conciliation meetings will go."

Upon hearing that Michael decides that he would up the stakes altogether. He knew a reporter from the Herald Sun newspaper and realizes that he would have to fight them all the way. Having also decided that he would risk it all, by seeking a ruling on their operating licenses, seeking to have special conditions inserted into their licensing conditions as infertility clinics. Maybe then they might be willing to hear them, conciliate with at least getting some compensation, maybe.

It is the 24th of July and Michael has been in his office at Long Real Estate. It is the most sullen mood Michael has felt in a long time.

Reading the letter quietly twice from James Smith the Victorian Government Solicitor.

In this James quoted that section 149(3) of the *Infertility Treatment Act* 1195 required that any application be made within 28 days of decision.

Apart from that information, Michael is now pessimistic after reading the letter that his application will be dismissed. What quietly alarms him the most which he did not share with Tania is that the Victorian Government Solicitor was instructed by the Infertility Treatment Authority to seek to recover all its legal costs in the event his application was struck out.

This is confirmed by the phone call he took on his mobile outside the office from Julie-Marie Baldwin, his assigned conciliation officer. Julie-Marie also informs him that the two clinics had a secret meeting with the Victorian Government Solicitor. This meeting was regarding his application to VCAT.

The letter writing campaign to members of parliament also came up. His recent conciliation meeting at the Health Services Commission office, which ended with no resolution, was also mentioned. The Victorian Solicitor was confident the application would be struck out because VCAT had no authority and no further review would have to take place.

Having typed letters to the Civil and Administrative Tribunal withdrawing his application Michael is going to fax it but decides to hold his nerve and makes a telephone call to Heather.

*Chapter 26*

Michael is in his car driving to Melbourne on the Mornington Peninsula freeway when he takes his fourth call of the morning.  It is only 8.15 am in the morning.

"Hello media star."

It was the voice of his good mate Graham on his mobile.

"How did you do it?  You're on today's page three of the Herald Sun news paper?  Mate, it means now everyone will know?"

Just then the buzzing sound of another call comes through.

Michael said to Graham, "I will ring you later."

"Hello, Michael Reid speaking."

"Hello, Michael Reid.  My name is Janice Koops I am a reporter, from channel 7's Today Tonight. We would like to do an exclusive interview with you together with your former wife."

"How did you get my mobile number?"

Michael is stunned that other media are interested.

"i rang your ex-wife Connie, she gave me your number."

"Oh I see."

"Yes and I would like you both to tell your part of this story which is featured on page 3 of today's Herald Sun newspaper."

Knowing he could get booked for speaking on his mobile Michael had to let Janice know that.

"I will have to call you back as I am driving and have to be in VCAT by 10 am."

Knowing now the media might be interested he continues on driving, still wondering where in the bloody hell this would all lead.

It is now 10.10 am and Michael is waiting nervously in the foyer outside the courtroom at the Victorian Civil & Administrative Tribunal at 55 King Street, Melbourne. Michael is a very nervous applicant as he waits to be called, for his Notice of Direction Hearing to begin.  He is wondering if the stares he was attracting from two good looking ladies are directed at him.  He is approached by a well dressed man who is accompanied by a young woman.

He asks if he is Michael Reid, and once Michael nods yes.

"Michael, I am James Smith the Victorian Government Solicitor who is representing the Infertility Treatment Authority. I have been instructed to seek the dismissal of your application for a review of the Infertility Treatment Authority decision, to reject your review application."

"I am aware of this."

Awaiting his next sentence.

"Well I will be seeking to have the tribunal have the ITA's legal costs, awarded against you, which are close to twelve thousand dollars."

Seeing Michael blink and the look of shock on his face, James continues, "If you withdraw your application now, I have been instructed not to seek the recovery of legal fees.  It's up to you."

All Michael could say without thinking is.

"See you in court."

It was then Michael knew he is not just seeking a medical review of the IVF treatment for him and Connie; he was fighting off financial ruin, too.

Feeling out of his depth, Michael listens as his VCAT Directions Hearing reference number G694/2002 is called by the clerk of the court.

"Is there a representative plus the applicant here this morning?" presiding VCAT senior member Jacqueline Russell asks.

Michael stands nervously.

"Your honor I the applicant Michael Reid am representing myself."

"Is there a representative for the Infertility Treatment Authority?"

Immediately James Smith stands up and speaks.

"James Smith from the Victorian Government Solicitors office, with my college Lindy Booth are representing the Infertility Treatment Authority this morning your honor."

Jacqueline Russell looks at Michael directly, before asking a question of the Victorian Government's Solicitor.
"I have before me a copy of the Infertility Treatment Act of 1995 and the section 149 of the act. Is this interpretation of section 149 the basis of the defence by the Infertility Treatment Authority?"
"Yes it is your honor as it clearly reads that only an affected party can seek to appear before the licensing committee."
At this Michael rises to speak but the senior member puts her hand up to indicate to Michael to wait.
"Those affected parties by the Infertility Treatment Act of 1995, definitions clearly do not include individuals or third parties."

This is said with confidence, by the ITA's legal representative.  After briefly reading the section of the Infertility Treatment Act, the senior member of the panel indicates Micheal to rise before the members.
"Mr Reid, if you would like to make a short summary of your application or seek to ask the legal representative of the Infertility Treatment Authority, any relevant questions with regards to your application for a hearings direction."
"I would your honor." Then, taking a deep breath and trying not to freeze up, Michael begins.
"Today I am seeking a ruling, to direct two clinics to do a full medical and ethical procedures review.  Seeing that it was IVF and the Infertility Treatment Authority is

the Victorian IVF patient's watchdog.  Today's ruling will enable me and my former wife to seek answers, on treatment and probable medical misdiagnosis that happened."

Then he asks the senior member a question while directing it at the legal team for the Infertility Treatment Authority.

"Am I and my former wife not affected parties under section 149s of the Infertility Treatment Authority?" "That is what today's, direction hearing will decide upon shortly but, before we do are there any further questions you have Mr Reid?"
"Not only that, I strongly argue that we are affected parties, in seeking a review of our medical care."  Then speaking further without being asked, Michael addresses everyone.
"You see, today's outcome started in 1995 when we began an IVF journey as a couple but ended as individuals.  Who were once close friends who have since parted ways but are not now seeking retribution but honest answers from our treating doctors without a battery of lawyers blocking our way."
After a moments silence, Jacqueline Russell proceeds on with the hearing.
"Mr Smith, do you have anything you would like to respond too or add before we give our findings?"
"Yes your honorable members, that I would remind those present that the Health Services Commission and the state Medical boards both have provisions for mediation and seeking redress for Mr Reid. The Infertility Treatment Authority does not have provisions under section 149s of the Infertility Treatment Act of 1995, to hear Mr Reid's application for a directions hearing today at VCAT."

After a brief pause, the senior member indicates to the clerk of the tribunal that the members are ready to give a verdict.

"Could both parties, please rise before the Tribunal."

Michael quickly stands up, unsure of what is to follow next.

It was then the senior member Jacqueline Russell announces.

"Mr Reid you are seeking a Directions Hearing today, to order a review of your medical care by the Infertility Treatment Authority. Unfortunately the Victorian Civil and Administrative Tribunal do not have the jurisdiction to order a review under Section 149s of the Infertility Treatment Act of 1995. The application is therefore refused."

With a smile of satisfaction, the solicitor for the Infertility Treatment Authority addresses the tribunal.

"The ITA is seeking to have court costs awarded against the applicant." With an immediate shake of her head senior member Jacqueline Russell responds.

"The tribunal has decided that each party is responsible for their own legal costs in regards to today's application."

This surprises the legal team for the ITA, but Michael exhales a silent, "Thank god."

Now Michael understands the stares and the general head turning his way. The Herald Sun and the Age newspaper plus two television stations are covering his direction hearing at VCAT. Suddenly he is being asked for some comments on his unsuccessful application by the news media. Being told where to stand and prepare himself for the questions he notices out of the corner of his sight, the senior member Jacqueline Russell watching and he thought she mouthed to him the word,
"Sorry."

"Michael, you must be disappointed by today's VCAT ruling dismissing your application against the Infertility Treatment Authority."

Seeing that the question is asked by the senior reporter Guy Stringer of the ABC news, Michael could not help himself but speak honestly.

"Yes I am, as it leaves current and former patients like us vulnerable to an IVF system which is run by specialists with vested interests."

It is the attractive lady news reporter who asked the next question.
"Mr Reid, what were you hoping to achieve today with your application before VCAT?"
"Truthfully, some answers to questions that bothered us then and now."

From the position of the cameraman Michael can see, it is a Channel 10 news reporter he is speaking too.

"Do you blame IVF for the failure of your marriage to your former wife?"
"The ongoing stress and the failed IVF attempts, it ended up being the weight around our necks. From which we could not cope and separated, but yes it was partly responsible."
Then the news reporter from the Herald Sun newspaper asks Michael,
"Will you be taking further court action in regards to your medical claims against the IVF clinics?"
"What I will be doing is lobbying to tighten control by government to ensure standards are uniform across this industry. I will also be calling for a medical ethics review and an independent body to oversee this industry."
He continues to speak from the heart to the media.

"Please understand that when the medical specialists tell you to play the game you do, they had us by the balls so to speak."

This brought laughter from the reporters so Michael adds.
"Better not put that in the news.  I am not sure if I will be able to continue court action; those costs are not my priority now, I will be seeking other avenues of redress."

With that the news reporters are satisfied they have enough for Michael's side of the story.  It was a news cameraman from channel 10 who asks.
"So where are the kids?"

Realizing the media wanted pictures of the kids to supplement the story.

"One's at home and the older boy is at daycare."

"We need to film them for the story, Michael."
"Well, you will have to come down to Rosebud. Say I will meet you on the foreshore opposite Boneo Road by 1.00 pm.  OK?"

With a nod of their heads the 10 news stations camera man says.
"1 pm will be fine; we both will need to be back at our stations by 3 pm to edit for the tonight's news."

"I'd better go then.  See you at Rosebud Foreshore at 1 pm."
It is then they film Michael walking away from court and suddenly Michael wants to run away like he had seen others do on television.  Tania is furious about the boys being filmed for the story when told.

*Chapter 27*

It is now November 12th 2002 at 1.30 pm and a second meeting is being held at the Health Services Commission in King Street Melbourne. At this meeting is the senior conciliator Ken Jackson who is visibly keen to get things smoothly underway. Michael immediately understands the media attention since July; with interviews on ABC radio have had a desired effect. Dr Heath is reluctantly seated at this second meeting.

There is a subdued tone of everyone's greeting, and strict formality shown. Everyone else, except Ken Jackson avoided eye contact. Michael keeps thinking it's "game on," as he waits for the chairperson, Ken Jackson, to start the meeting.

Having recently moved to Wangaratta with Tania and five of the children, Tania urges him that morning to accept any offer if put on the table. For the first time in nearly four years his morality was the focus. The media crusade, against his IVF experience is mentioned at the meeting. Despite self justification, even now he too wishes sometimes that,

"It was all over."

Even though his action against the Infertility Treatment Authority had been dismissed by VCAT. Michael is surprised at seeing Bonnie Stewart sitting next to Dr Heath. It is Bonnie Stewart who asks to speak first to Michael directly.

"Mr Reid, you are aware that your media campaign is having an effect on couples undertaking IVF in the state of Victoria."

Taken aback at first, Michael responds after leaning forward towards Bonnie Stewart.

"Wow, sorry, I didn't realize asking for an investigation and getting to the truth was such a big problem for you all."

With a firm jaw with glances at the doctors Bonnie explains.

"That is not what I am speaking about, Mr Reid; the media attention is having effect.  Some couples are delaying their IVF treatment."

"So I'm bad for business then."

With that said, the open hostility towards Michael is evident to by all.

It is then Dr Heath finally speaks to Michael.

"Do you know or care about how many couples both Dr Sloob and I have helped?  Do you think that your ill-informed media stunts are helpful?"  Thankfully, Ken Jackson retakes control of the meeting.  Having the questions rephrased makes Michael pause before answering.

"I can't answer those questions.  All I know it's nearly four years with no proper medical response or offers of compensation."

It is then Professor Clark who speaks.

"That is not correct.  I personally wrote a four page medical reply to the Health Services Commissioner last year."

"That might be so but you never answered any of my main points I raised about our treatment."

Again Michael can see his nostrils flare as Professor Clark replies.

"I will not entertain questions from someone about infertility.  Whose knowledge would not even pass as a first year medical student's."

"So why are you here then?"

"They are here to finalize this conciliation between yourself and Dr Heath, as directed by the Health Services Commissioner."

Ken Jackson replies for the clinics, looking directly at Michael now.

"I don't see or feel any conciliation so far, so what about compensation?"

It is Dr Heath who shakes her head and mumbles something that Michael does not hear.  Looking closely, he can see tears in her eyes.  It is Bonnie Stewart from the Infertility Treatment Authority who asks the final question.
"How much would it take to settle this matter Michael?"
"If we were in America, eight hundred thousand would do, but all we want is fifty thousand to settle this complaint."
Quickly Michael realizes that was a mistake, as all three doctors, indicates to Robin Marks to end the meeting. Only Bonnie Stewart and Ken Jackson wanted the talking to continue.

Now realizing his mistake, all Michael wants to do is get back to his car before the meter expires. He is aware that during his three hour drive home, he will be cursing his stupidity.

## Chapter 28

It is now 22[th] of March 2003; Michael is sitting down on his bed in their Wangaratta home, reading the most recent letter from the Health Services Commission regarding his most recent telephone call.

"I promise, Tania, this is the very last trip I am making to Melbourne to talk to them.  Look, I know that you warned me that this would drag on but I promise it's nearly over."

He can tell from her body language that she is not happy with him making the trip.  In truth, Michael is unhappy to again drive to Melbourne while taking a whole day away from home. The cost of petrol and parking also is a pain also.

"Look, I have had enough. We moved up here to Wangaratta, to get away from Connie and Rosebud."

As he moves to hold Tania, with a kiss on the head, Michael promises.

"If they don't offer to conciliate now I will drop it, I promise."

Tania walks out of the bedroom as Michael again rereads all of the recent correspondence from the Victorian Minister for Health and the Health Services Commission. He feels very glum about the strict confidential clauses saying he could not talk to the press.  This is his last roll of the dice as the news media indicated unless he has something substantively new.  It would be hard to justify continuing coverage of his campaign.

The meeting is at the offices of the Infertility Treatment Authority. The complete board of the ITA is in attendance.

"While respecting the board's final decision, I as CEO have a duty to explore other avenues, as outlined by the current business plan as approved by the board."

Going on further Bonnie Stewart explains to the chairman.

"Look I have meet this Michael Reid, the one who has the specialists jumping at shadows. All he wanted was a layman's explanation of what happened, plus his money back."

It is then the chairman Professor Harvey Barton intervenes.

"Bonnie, the ITA plus medical hospital systems have a long standing sound policy of not offering compensation unless recommended by our lawyers or damages awarded by a superior court."

"I am not challenging the current policy as directed by the board and the Victorian health department. What I am challenging is that in the financial years 1999/2000 our legal fees were $3,897.00 dollars and in 2001/2002 the authority's legal fees were $32,587.00."

This gives pause for thought by Professor Barton who asks aloud making eye contact with the CEO.

"So what are you recommending, to the board?"

"That the board gives me in principle the room to start talking to the Princess Margret's and Alpha/Stork about the possibility of offering a settlement, which would remain confidential. That Princess Margret's pay the majority and both Alpha/Stork and the authority pay any balance. If I can convince Mr Reid to a lower figure so that the medical insurance lawyers don't have to know about it. It will be a win/win for everyone."

With some quiet nodding from three board members Professor Barton says, "Go on."

"Look, I must say as chief executive officer that all of us have taken on some important lessons from this. Under current legislation we are duty bound as office holders to uphold the legislation as defined by the Infertility Treatment Act of 1995. What we can do as a priority is approve the legal representatives for any clinics who not only act in the best interests of the clinics but within accepted ethical legal standards."

It was then the only female board member asks Bonnie a question. "Is this still regarding Mr Reids case or something else?  I also see from reading this agenda before me other points regarding IVF directorships, the recommended company ownership structures plus Australian andrology testing standards."

"In truth? Yes to both Susan. I believe that combative legal defence against Mr Reid is being over used.  But IVF clinics having defence lawyers, whose other major client is vigorously defending the Catholic Church needs to be also reviewed."

Now, wanting to move on, Professor Barton asks.

"If we could have a show of hands later as we move on to the next item, as listed on the agenda." All eyes in the room are lowered as they carefully read the next reform agenda for the Infertility Treatment Authority as recommended by Professor Harry Pollard.

It is just after 11 am on Thursday 25th of March 2003. Ms Bonnie Stewart, the Chief Executive Officer, is seated at her desk in her office of the Infertility Treatment Authority.  It was a lot easier than she thought it would be.  Bonnie was very surprised by the listening ears of the general manager for Alpha/Stork IVF.

The positive feedback from Princess Margret's financial controller. Both have promised to ring her back with a definite reply by 4.00 pm this afternoon. Having quickly established, yesterday, that if both clinics kept any confidential settlement below $14,000.00 each. That legal vulture Robin Marks could not overrule a confidential settlement by all parties. Alpha/Stork were the most positive as their general manager pointed out that each time they engage the medical legal lawyers was very expensive. The financial controller felt that it could be possible to reach agreement on a figure by the end of the day. His main concern would be keeping it strictly confidential in a public health system. When Bonnie pointed out there was to be binding confidentiality on Mr Reid with the three parties suing for damages if a breach occurred. Scribbling down notes to dictate to her receptionist Bonnie wished she had acted earlier. Firstly to save the ITA from any adverse publicity and the Victorian tax payer.

The most unsettling feeling she keeps is that she does feel great empathy for couples who fail to achieve their wishes using Victorian IVF clinics.

Plus the uncomfortable knowledge that Mr Reid was half correct in that the clinics and andrology laboratories should not be wholly owned or controlled by the treating medical specialists.

Now to put a confidential settlement on the table tomorrow. Without the lawyers interfering, plus Mr Reid accepting it.

*Chapter 29*

Michael is driving along the Hume Highway on Wednesday 31st March 2003. The time is 10.40 am and he is heading for his meeting at the Health Services Commission at 1.30 pm in Melbourne.

It is not until he drives past Wallan, on the Hume highway that Michael is able to tune in any Melbourne radio stations he liked listening too.

Using the enforced silence so he can think and hopefully plan what to say at today's meeting. Since having moved to Wangaratta, Tania is very keen to put the past behind them. Both of them have started attending church again at her prompting as his combative attacking style was starting to wear thin on his wife.

At first Michael is very upbeat as John Farnham song "Playing to Win" is played, which he sings very loudly as he drives along. This stops when he notices a family group placing two children's crosses beside the freeway. Then the song which Connie often played, "I just want to make love to you," by Heart comes on. His mood changes dramatically as he remembers what they all had been through. Vivid memories of his own long denied anger and the pain it caused his family bring him to tears.

Driving into Crown Casino's multi-storey car park, Michael Jackson's "Man in the Mirror" comes on the radio.

After parking the car, Michael searches through the glove box for the bible tract that Tania placed in there.

After finding it, he re-prays The Sinners Prayer. He knows he IS going to apologize to Dr Bronwyn Heath personally today. Any thoughts of a final settlement he had for Connie and himself driving down the Hume highway with were now three hundred kilometers away.

It is now 1.30 and Michael is seated in a meeting room in the Health Services Commission and is waiting for the meeting to begin.  Feelings of guilt and shame, nearly overcome him as he waits for the conciliation meeting to begin.  Then he notices that Dr Heath and Professor Barton are speaking easily with Bonnie Stewart from the ITA.

The body language is also more positive and even Ken Jackson the chair of the meeting, seemed to pick up on it.  He also notices that they quickly sit down when Robin Marks from Conner/Coop & Co, their medical legal lawyers, enters the room.  Everybody knows this will be the last conciliation meeting between them today.

Maybe just maybe, as Michael rubs his face he hopes that a proper explanation will finally be given.  So that is the plan, ask medical questions without the aggressive attitude. Ken Jackson's summary of the conciliation process was factual and to the formula laid out for conciliation. Again Michael is asked to ask a question that strictly related to his complaints to the Health Services Commission.

"My opening question, well it's not all a question, is directed to Dr Heath. I never did properly thank you for trying to help Connie and myself in having a baby but I have to know.  What went wrong?"

Nodding at first before answering, Dr Heath replies,

"Michael I don't know, God knows."

Taken aback by the language, Michael answers while examining those words.

"God knows. Well I do know God and I am not bringing him into it.  I call myself a Christian, not a very good one as people now know.   It was memories of the eggs that didn't turn into babies that hurt my faith. It's also given me some lifelong personal wisdom, my IVF journey."

Ken Jackson starts to speak before Michael continues on speaking.

"I do not hold anything against IVF science; it's just that it was not the right option for us as a couple.  I know how many times I masturbated into those jars, but you all here need to know that I was never a wanker."

Bonnie Stewart notices that Michael is not shying away from these words, uncomfortable as it is for everyone listening in the room.

"So Michael, what is it you really want from us today?"

She is about to open a file in front of her to give to Michael, when Robin Marks reached over and places his right hand on the file.  With a shake of his head he says,

"Don't, not now."

"Well, I was hoping for a medical explanation but,  Dr Heath, you just gave it to me. God knows. Yes God knows. Please forgive my stupid actions against the clinics.  That is all I can say I guess."

Now Ken Jackson spoke before anyone else can,

"So are you now satisfied with that answer from Dr Heath?"

"Yes and I now no longer wish to seek any compensation through conciliation.  I honestly apologize, to Dr Heath personally for any distress.  I am now sorry that it came to this. I also want to thank the Health Services Commission and you Ken for everything, you have done."

"Well if no one has anything further to add, I will call this meeting to a close and just so everyone is aware the Health Services Commission will be writing to all parties to confirm the end of the conciliation process. I thank you all for your time today."

It is Bonnie Stewart from the ITA who shakes her head in disbelief. Michael rings Tania outside on the street and tells her,

'It's all over.  I'm coming home."

*Chapter 30*

It is a Sunday in late July 2003. Michael is with Tania and their boys at the ground floor cafe "Heathers" in Punt Road Richmond.

"Hope you found my place all right. Welcome to my new cafe. I have some very special ladies who want to meet you."

"Yes we did find it, I watched this building being built, and I'll never forget it."

"Would you like a coffee and a drink for the kids? It's on me."

"Thank you. That's very kind of you Heather but first I need directions to where is the nearest parents change room toilet?"

Michael has been holding on to going himself and he knew his youngest needed his nappy changed by the smell. Given his directions, he also now notices that Alpha/Stork IVF has moved from across the road. When Michael returns with a settled son Lewis, he notices Tania happily talking to a woman he had never seen before. Giving him his coffee, Tania speaks to Michael.

"This is Sam and she is a big fan of what you did to the clinics."

"Nice to meet you Sam, what did I exactly do?"

"Don't you know that your VCAT case? You also nearly halted all IVF in Victoria."

"No, what do you mean by bringing IVF to a halt in Victoria, Sam?"

"We all know that if you had been successful in your VCAT case to get your case reviewed, all IVF south of Albury New South Wales would have been suspended. The senior specialists were very concerned.

"Really? Why?"

"We have been told that the Victorian minister of Health was going to convene a departmental inquiry, into the testing standards.  Plus the ownership structures of clinics by IVF specialists"

As he takes that news in and sips his coffee Heather comes over holding a little girl about 12 months old.
"This is my granddaughter Jackie and, here comes my daughter Brook.

Do you remember her Michael, from Alpha/Stork IVF?"
A tall woman in her early thirties approaches, Michael remembers with a slight laugh.
"We all remember your mishaps when you tried to masturbate."
"I remember those times all too well," is all Michael can say to that.
'Sam is Brook's partner and Jackie is their daughter." Now the flash of realization hits Michael. The rainbow colors, Heather's, IVF knowledge, her helping his media campaign.  He has to laugh also.
"I didn't know," is all he can think of to say. It is Sam who then asked Michael some more questions.
"Michael, did you know that the clinics were going to offer you a confidential settlement but it never happened. Do you know why?"
Looking down now at Tania, Michael responds shaking his head.
"I didn't know of any settlement offer, it was never put to me."
It was Brook who filled them in on what happened.
"It was very confidential at the clinic but some of us knew that they wanted to keep your case quiet so other couples didn't ask similar questions.  Your case changed the way couples are informed of treatment options and infertility levels."
"I didn't know that either."

"The specialists were really relieved when you dropped your complaints but the Infertility Treatment Authority pushed through new regulations with uniformity standards across the medical profession."

"I didn't know that also."
"We know."

All three say together laughing.

*THE OTHER MAN*

*The Other Man could control and shout*
*This Man knows what it's all about,*
*The Other Man would behold his right*
*This Man is under the light,*
*The Other Man has strong arms and legs*
*This Man has strength from within,*
*The Other Man was distant and moody*
*This Man is close and content,*
*The Other Man would refuse to confess*
*This Man knows he's not alone,*
*The Other Man is trapped in his anger*
*This Man is freed from his bondage,*
*The Other Man has addictions he hides*
*This Man guards his heart and mind,*
*The Other Man would blame his wife*
*This man knows, she is the love for his life,*
*The Other Man could not let go*
*This Man knew it was vital so,*
*The Other Man was full of pride*
*This Man knows he's under grace,*
*The Other Man has gone away*
*This Man is here to stay.*

*This is the poem I wrote and read out aloud to over 90 motorcyclists to Ms Rosie Batty, (2015 Australian of the year) on 1st March 2014 at the Tyabb cricket ground.*

*I am proud of holding  the very first public event after Luke Batty's tragic death.*

*I informed Rosie after the service, that the poem above was written about myself. Rosie nodded that she already knew.*